"YOU'RE STARING, CARRIE."

She blinked. "You're right. I like the view."

"I feel the same way," he said. "I'm so hungry for you that I wonder if my appetite will ever be satisfied."

She'd never had this kind of a conversation with a man before, and she didn't know the rules—if there were any rules. Without considering the wisdom of her actions, she moved across the width of the couch to sit beside him.

He slid his arm around her shoulders and tugged. When she glanced up at him, she nearly drowned in the depths of his eyes.

No man had ever looked at her with such unabashed desire, and no man had ever evoked an answering desire within her heart and body. She sucked in a ragged breath.

His gaze narrowed. "What are you thinking about right now?"

"That we don't need that fire tonight. I'm already quite hot."

WHAT ARE *LOVESWEPT* ROMANCES?

They are stories of true romance and touching emotion. We believe those two very important ingredients are constants in our highly sensual and very believable stories in the LOVESWEPT *line. Our goal is to give you, the reader, stories of consistently high quality that may sometimes make you laugh, sometimes make you cry, but are always fresh and creative and contain many delightful surprises within their pages.*

Most romance fans read an enormous number of books. Those they truly love, they keep. Others may be traded with friends and soon forgotten. We hope that each LOVESWEPT *romance will be a treasure—a "keeper." We will always try to publish*

LOVE STORIES YOU'LL NEVER FORGET
BY AUTHORS YOU'LL ALWAYS REMEMBER

The Editors

Loveswept® 784

DANGEROUS SURRENDER

LAURA TAYLOR

BANTAM BOOKS
NEW YORK · TORONTO · LONDON · SYDNEY · AUCKLAND

DANGEROUS SURRENDER
A Bantam Book / April 1996

ISBN 0-553-44525-1

Published simultaneously in the United States and Canada

Bantam Books are published by Bantam Books, a division of Bantam Doubleday Dell Publishing Group, Inc. Its trademark, consisting of the words "Bantam Books" and the portrayal of a rooster, is Registered in U.S. Patent and Trademark Office and in other countries. Marca Registrada. Bantam Books, 1540 Broadway, New York, New York 10036.

PRINTED IN THE UNITED STATES OF AMERICA

OPM 0 9 8 7 6 5 4 3 2 1

For Caroline and Brett,
with love and best wishes

ONE

Carrie Forbes stood in line at the bank and waited her turn for the next available teller. Her gaze snagged and held on a stranger who was talking to the bank manager, her curiosity and appreciation of the man's masculinity concealed by the dark glasses she wore. He was tall, sun-bronzed, and not at all handsome in the classic sense of the word.

Rugged was the best way to describe him, Carrie finally decided as she watched the two men shake hands and exchange a few final words. The unknown man turned, offering a more complete view of himself as the men parted company. Her gaze skimmed over his thick, dark hair, angular features, broad shoulders, and sturdy body.

An unmistakable air of authority emanated from him as his long-legged stride carried him into the lobby. His innate confidence showed in the powerful lines of his body and in the steadiness of his gaze when his footsteps slowed.

He looked directly at her, his gaze sweeping over her. Her breath caught in her throat. She felt her pulse pick up speed, the sudden escalation taking her by surprise.

A harsh shout rang out, shattering the churchlike stillness of the bank. Carrie flinched, then turned to search for the cause of the sharp sound still echoing in the air.

Firecrackers, a string of them, followed a heartbeat later. Confused, she searched for the source and watched with shock as three armed men burst into the lobby.

One of the men uttered a guttural command at the stunned customers and bank employees. "Everybody down on the floor! Now!"

Her mind snapped a picture of the three unmasked men, a horrifying, almost surreal mental photo of faces filled with deadly intent. Carrie recoiled, but her body refused to honor the orders issued by her mind, despite instincts honed by an event in her past that urged her to flee, urged her to seek safety in the face of the madness unfolding around her. Uncertainty and a brand of fear that she hadn't known in many years paralyzed her.

Strong hands suddenly settled on her shoulders, jerking her backward. Her purse thudded as it hit the floor.

Carrie cried out, responding to the insanity of the moment. She couldn't help herself.

"Quiet!" one of the robbers snarled as he swung his semiautomatic weapon in her direction.

The hands on her shoulders gripped her even more tightly. She lost her balance.

Gunfire erupted across the lobby. A woman screamed. A man crumpled to the floor.

Wild-eyed, Carrie realized that he'd been shot. She struggled with renewed purpose to free herself, twisting, resisting, in spite of the futility of the endeavor.

"I told you people to hit the deck! Heads down!"

The hands on her shoulders lifted. She drew in a strangled breath and lurched forward. Arms snaked around her middle like cords of steel, anchoring her against hard muscle and dragging her backward yet again. She stiffened, outrage, panic, and adrenaline running rampant through her bloodstream.

"Don't fight me, dammit!" a voice whispered harshly into her ear. "I'm trying to help you."

Carrie sagged suddenly. Without understanding why, she accepted his explanation. Without wondering why, she also connected his voice to the stranger she'd noticed in conversation with the bank manager just moments earlier.

He swung her around, propelling her away from the center of the lobby. Her sunglasses flew off her face and clattered to the floor. A cream-colored wall swirled before her eyes, the nondescript painting positioned on it a blur. Bullets suddenly penetrated the pastoral scene, riddling frame, canvas, and wall plaster in a garish pattern. She watched in horror as the painting self-destructed.

Jerked off her feet, Carrie landed on her knees, then crashed sideways onto the floor. Powerful hands flattened her slender body against the wall. As the man who'd grabbed her stretched out on his side beside her, she gasped for breath. She inhaled the choking rain of plaster dust and gagged on it.

"Listen up, all of you!"

Her gaze was riveted to the man towering over their prone bodies. She breathed shallowly, trying not to cough.

Someone nearby moaned, the sound replete with pain. Disbelief flowed through her like charges of electricity. Her heart raced, threatening to jump out of her chest.

"Cooperate and you'll live. Give us a hard time, it's your funeral."

The armed man turned away.

One of his cohorts shouted, "Get that damn vault open now!"

He punctuated his order with gunfire. A light fixture exploded. Slivers of glass showered down from the high ceiling to litter the floor.

Carrie shivered violently.

"Stay calm," a low voice urged.

She blinked, then focused on the tension-filled features of the man who'd dragged her out of the teller line. For some inexplicable reason she sensed that she could trust him.

"Do you understand what I'm saying?" he whispered.

Carrie nodded. Badly shaken, she couldn't control the reflexive shudders still rippling through her. She searched his face, taking in hard angles, intense, dark eyes, and the aura of steely confidence she'd noted a few moments earlier. She wondered then what kind of man willingly used his own body as a barrier to protect a woman he didn't know.

A decent man, she decided as she stared at him. A man of honor. It occurred to her that she hadn't known many in her thirty-five years.

A baby whimpered. Carrie ground her teeth together, quelling the impulse to respond. The baby whimpered once more. The mother tried to quiet it with soothing words, but the stark fear edging the woman's voice simply served to escalate the child's distress.

Carrie lifted her head, her response to the baby too instinctive to contain any longer.

The man beside her grabbed her hand.

She glimpsed the warning in his expression, lowered her head, and pressed her cheek to the cold marble floor.

A gunshot echoed in the next instant. He jerked, as though slapped unexpectedly.

She felt his hold on her hand go limp. Carrie heard the harsh breath he sucked in. She watched him sink his front teeth into his lower lip. Shock lanced through her. He'd been shot trying to protect her.

She wanted to scream her fury at such senseless violence. She bit her tongue to silence herself instead. Grasping his hand, she held on to him and silently willed him to open his eyes.

He finally did.

She saw the pain she'd inadvertently caused as she held his gaze. Regret pooled inside her, nearly swamping her fragile emotional control.

She exhaled shakily.

"Let's get moving!"

Carrie cringed, then held so still that her muscles felt knotted. Her heartbeat threatened to deafen her. As she gazed at the face of her protector and tried to calm herself, the sound of footsteps racing across the lobby floor penetrated the roaring in her ears.

"The cops are on their way! Hurry it up!"

She whispered a silent prayer for deliverance. For life.

One of the robbers paused as his companions headed for the lobby side door. He delivered a final command. "Stay put or you'll die."

Silence reigned, a kind of stunned silence that seemed to last forever. Carrie counted every breath she took.

"They're gone," an unfamiliar voice finally announced. "Someone call for an ambulance. We've got seriously wounded people over here."

A woman began to sob.

Others spoke as they got to their feet, hysteria tinging their voices.

Carrie struggled up from her prone position on the floor and into a seated position. Her companion rolled onto his back, clutching his arm.

"Let me help you," she pleaded.

"Give me a minute," he said through gritted teeth.

She knelt at his side, frantic for him to be all right. He'd saved her life. How did you thank someone for that kind of behavior? she wondered.

Although aware of the activity around her as bank patrons and employees assisted the wounded and crying, Carrie couldn't tear her eyes from the man sprawled on the floor in front of her. He became her sole focus. She touched his cheek, an unconscious need to assure herself that he would be all right dominating her thoughts and senses. His skin was warm, vital, and she exhaled raggedly.

He opened his eyes. Beautiful eyes the color of dark cocoa, beautiful in spite of the pain glazing them.

Carrie removed her hand from his cheek, closing it into a fist to still the shaking of her fingers. "I'm so sorry," she whispered.

"I'm all right," he managed to say as he continued to cradle his arm against his body.

"No, you're not."

The expression on his face told her that he

wasn't accustomed to being contradicted. She might have smiled under other circumstances, but not now. Now she felt like weeping. But there wasn't time for that kind of self-indulgence, she reminded herself.

Working together, they got him into a seated position. He leaned against the wall, his gaze scanning the bank lobby before returning to her face.

Carrie dragged her sweatshirt, which she'd pulled on over her unitard after exercise class, over her head. Rusty first-aid training skills kicked in. She tore the sleeve of his once-white shirt away from his injured upper arm, gritting her teeth when she saw the blood still flowing from the wound. Using the sleeves of her sweatshirt, she fashioned a tourniquet to slow the bleeding.

Easing into a seated position at his side, she slipped an arm around him. When he stiffened, she urged, "Lean against me. Help should be here any minute now."

He flashed a look at her that she didn't understand, then settled heavily against her. She felt the tension in his muscular body with every breath he took.

"Thanks."

"Thank *you*," Carrie managed.

"For what?" he asked, his voice sharp-edged.

"For helping me. I couldn't believe what was happening."

"No one could," he muttered. "If I hadn't seen them, I wouldn't have, either."

"I saw them too. Their faces, I mean."

He peered at her, probing her features. "The surveillance cameras probably caught their performance as well. Stupid of them not to conceal their faces."

She nodded, leaned her head back against the wall, and worked at collecting her scattered wits before she spoke again. "I'm Carrie Forbes."

"Brian York," he offered.

She didn't miss the hoarseness of his voice. "Can I get you a glass of water?"

He shook his head. "Just sit tight."

The welcome sound of sirens penetrated the haze settling over her.

"You'll have help soon."

"Isn't that what you're doing?"

"You need more than my outdated first-aid skills."

"I'm fine. It's just a flesh wound."

Shocked by his dismissive remark, she reminded him, "You were shot. Because of . . . if I hadn't . . ."

"Don't! I'm alive. That's all the counts as far as I'm concerned."

She paled, the frantic scene unfolding around them in the lobby reminding her that others might not be alive by the end of the day.

"You aren't responsible for what happened to me, and I'll be all right," he said.

She nodded, relief nearly choking her. "Fortunately."

He shifted against her, then winced. His eyes fell closed.

She tightened her hold on him. "Try not to move."

Police personnel and paramedics rushed into the lobby just seconds later. Carrie closed her eyes, a tremor passing through her. She suddenly hated the sound of footsteps on marble.

"You okay?" he asked.

"Delayed reaction, I suspect."

"You're allowed."

The reality of what had just happened somersaulted in her stomach. A wave of dizziness followed. She closed her eyes once again in an effort to steady herself.

"Don't pass out on me."

She concentrated on the sound of his deep voice. The impulse to faint passed. "I hate feeling vulnerable."

"Normal reaction."

Too normal for me, she realized, recalling a past she'd never been able to outrun. Feeling helpless was something she loathed, but she didn't want to dwell on why. Especially not now. "Perhaps," she conceded.

A paramedic dropped to his knees in front of them and conducted a quick inspection of Brian's injury. "We've got another gunshot over here," he called over his shoulder to a coworker. "It looks minor, though."

Brian brushed the man's hands aside. "The bullet passed through. Deal with the others. I'll wait my turn."

"Where'd you take your training?" the clean-cut young man asked, his tone good-natured as he carefully confirmed the existence of an exit wound and then examined the makeshift tourniquet.

"A variety of places, all courtesy of the army."

Looking grim, the paramedic nodded. "Me too. Desert Storm. Tourniquet looks good. Who did it?"

"The lady."

The young man glanced at her. "Need a job?"

Carrie almost managed an answering smile. Almost.

"Tom! He's arresting on me."

Brian settled back against the wall. "Go on. We both know I'm not in any danger."

The paramedic surged to his feet. "It'll be a few minutes."

Carrie understood the need to prioritize, but it was at odds with her desire to have Brian York taken care of as quickly as possible. "You need help. I wish I knew what to do."

"It could have been a lot worse."

The fact that he was right didn't make the reality that he'd been shot any easier for her to bear. "I still can't believe this has happened."

"Believe it."

A sob tore through her as she stared at her hands.

He shrugged free of her encircling arm and looped his uninjured arm around her shoulders. "Lean on me, Carrie Forbes. Don't hold in your feelings. Cry if you need to. It'll help."

She shook her head, blinking back the emotion flooding her eyes. He'd been shot, and he was offering her comfort. She didn't know how to respond, so she simply voiced a conclusion she'd come to long ago. "Tears don't solve anything."

Carrie felt the sweep of his inspecting gaze and lifted her chin, determined to control herself. She peered at him, looking more vulnerable than she realized.

"Is that experience talking?" he asked quietly.

The compassion she saw in his dark eyes bewildered and startled her.

"Is it?" he pressed.

"Perhaps."

"You're a lot stronger than you look, aren't you?"

She inhaled sharply, unnerved by his insight. She'd learned to be strong, learned to get through a crisis on sheer nerve when she had to.

When she didn't respond, he pulled her closer. She rested her head on his shoulder, grateful for his physical strength and compassion. Consciously disconnecting from the flurry of activity still taking place in the bank lobby, Carrie inhaled the blending scents of a citrusy aftershave and the faint muskiness of his skin. She savored the warmth emanating from his powerful body, and for a moment she longed to lose herself in it and him.

A man clad in a three-piece suit, the jacket unbuttoned, approached them. Carrie stared at the badge dangling from his belt loop and the weapon holstered under his arm as he squatted down in front of them.

"I'm Detective Landis. We'll need statements once the medical types take care of you. So will the feds when they arrive, since this is a federally insured bank."

Carrie and Brian both nodded.

"You two together?"

"We are now," Brian York answered.

"How about some chairs?" he asked them. "That floor can't be too comfortable."

Brian shook his head. "Not necessary."

Feeling like a visitor to the Twilight Zone, Carrie watched one of the injured bank patrons being loaded onto a gurney for transport via ambulance to the hospital. He was quickly wheeled out. A paramedic crouched over the man as he administered CPR.

I'm going to learn how to do that, she promised herself. She refused to feel or view herself as helpless or useless ever again.

"Miss?"

She met the detective's gaze.

"Can I do anything for you?"

Carrie shook her head, too numb to speak.

The detective made a final comment as he straightened. Carrie heard the sound of his voice, but the words got lost as she experienced another wave of shock. It rolled over her, leaving disorientation and disbelief in its wake. She pressed her fingertips to her temples and massaged the ache throbbing there.

"Take some deep breaths," Brian urged.

She did. They helped.

"Talk to me," he said.

"About what?" Carrie lowered her hand to her lap and glanced at Brian.

"Anything. Yourself."

She heard the pain in his voice, and she recognized his need for a distraction; recognized her own as well. She made herself talk, made herself say the first thing that popped into her head. "I was born on an airplane."

"Say that again."

"My mother gave birth to me on a flight between New York and London."

He chuckled, the sound like rustling sheaves of old parchment. "Interesting and unusual."

"It's true. No one ever believes me until they see my birth certificate."

"Does it list the altitude?"

"Exactly."

"Tell me more."

"I . . . love cotton candy, puppies, and taking walks on the beach."

"What about hot dogs at the ballpark?"

"With plenty of mustard and relish."

"What about onions?"

"Pass."

He lifted her hand and inspected her ring finger. "You're not married. Why?"

Startled, she glanced at him. "Do you always ask such personal questions?"

"Hardly ever, but I don't get shot every day, either."

She nodded, understanding the path his mind had taken. Her own felt absolutely fragmented at the moment. "I was engaged, but we ended the relationship a long time ago."

"I was married." He shifted, exhaling heavily. The sound spoke of failure and regret. "Any children?"

"No," she whispered.

He studied her, his gaze narrowing. "You want them, though."

She reluctantly nodded. "Maybe someday." The admission cost her, because she doubted that she'd ever have any. Seriously doubted it.

"You should."

What a bizarre conversation, she thought. "Really?"

"You're a loving person."

"How can you tell?"

As she waited for his answer Carrie thought about the countless times her former fiancé had accused her of not feeling anything at all. The Ice

Queen, he'd called her. Even though she knew he'd been wrong, his insensitivity still haunted her when her defenses were down.

"Your touch," he said as his hand traveled soothingly back and forth across her shoulder. "You're very gentle."

Bemused, she stared up at him, registering yet again the angular contours of his face. His eyes were dark, bottomless pools of intensity. She glimpsed pain that wasn't just physical, understanding based on personal hardship.

Suddenly sucked down into the undertow of her own emotions, Carrie felt defenseless. This man saw too much. This man understood too much. He unnerved her. Caution flags suddenly unfurled in her head. Still, she felt drawn to him. Why? she wondered. Why this man?

"I'm serious," he insisted.

"You sound serious," she conceded warily.

"I'm not a threat, Carrie Forbes."

She frowned, because she sensed that he could be quite threatening under certain circumstances. A voice in her head suggested that he might also be the kind of man a woman could count on and trust in a relationship.

Startled by the ludicrous leap her mind had just taken, Carrie reminded herself that she'd once thought that about the man she'd almost married.

She looked away, unwilling to respond to his assurance that he posed no threat to her. She knew deep down that he did, because he'd forced her to acknowledge the hope still lodged in her heart—hope that someone would love her for herself. Hope that she would feel able to express love—freely, unconditionally, and without fear. Hope Carrie believed that she'd banished as a girlish fantasy long ago.

TWO

Brian didn't press Carrie any further. The expression on her face told him that he'd already gone too far.

Even though he didn't grasp the reasons for them, he recognized the walls she'd erected around herself for what they were. He had his own. Hers were too obvious to overlook. What he couldn't ignore, though, was the driving need within himself to scale them.

He realized that he must have sounded like a fool when he'd said he wasn't a threat to her, but the urge to reassure her had come out of nowhere, shocking him, clearly shocking her. Studying her profile, Brian closed his free hand into a fist and refrained from acting on the impulse to trail his fingertips across her cheek.

Her skin, which was a perfect counterpoint to the rich auburn tones of her thick, shoulder-length hair, reminded him of transparent silk. Brian fought a fierce inner battle for self-control in the moments that followed, because he wanted to touch her in other ways. Intimately. Tenderly. Completely. Passionately.

The desire to possess and explore her rocked him. He immediately credited it to the violent events that had just taken place, the instinctive need to celebrate their survival, and an unexpected brand of sensory heat that had evolved within him during the minutes in which their lives had hung in the balance.

Brian York knew better than to complicate his life, because experience had taught him bitter lessons about emotion-based relationships. Still, there was something about this particular woman that spoke to the self-imposed emotional isolation of his own life in recent years, spoke to the regret he still felt, the sense of having failed at a relationship he'd once assumed was mutually satisfying.

His ex-wife, however, had made it clear that he'd failed—big time.

The paramedic who'd examined him earlier approached them. Brian silently welcomed the distraction from the path of his conflicted thoughts.

"Let's get you two taken care of now, shall we?"

Brian jerked a nod at the paramedic, eased free of Carrie, and got to his feet. The pain caused by the gunshot wound had faded to a dull throbbing.

He wanted it dealt with, and he wanted to get out of the bank. He felt caged, and he hated the feeling.

"Where do you want me?" Brian asked.

The paramedic gestured to a grouping of chairs situated nearby. "How about over there?"

Brian hesitated, then glanced down at Carrie. He extended his hand to her. Her momentary indecision as she stared up at him infused him with the kind of regret that invariably precedes rejection.

She didn't reject him, however. Reaching up to take his proffered hand, she let him help her to her feet.

Brian felt both relief and confusion. Their connection, forged by crisis and severely strained now, mattered to him, mattered too much.

He gripped her hand as they silently walked to a carpeted area on the perimeter of the lobby that contained several chairs, a love seat, an assortment of tree-sized potted plants, and an oak desk now riddled with bullet holes. Brian didn't release her once they were seated side by side on the small couch.

The paramedic cut away the sleeve of his shirt, tested the mobility of his arm, took his blood pressure, and then reexamined the bullet wound. "I'll prep you for the ER attending physician at Mercy General," he said. "You may need a few stitches."

"Is there anything I can do to help?" Carrie asked, breaking her silence.

The young man winked at her. "You *are* helping. Just hold on to him. He's probably as tough as he looks, but you never know about these big guys. When they keel over, they tend to land real hard."

"I'm not going to the hospital," Brian announced, suddenly annoyed that they were talking around him. "Do whatever needs to be done now."

Carrie gripped his hand more tightly.

He felt and saw her worry, even though she refused to meet his gaze. "I'm fine," he said quietly, unable to ignore her distress.

She nodded, but she didn't ease her hold on him.

"I hope you'll reconsider your decision, sir. You really should be seen in the ER. I might miss something important. We can transport you by ambulance, or you can get there under your own steam."

Brian shook his head. "You know what you're doing. This is a nuisance wound, nothing more." He winced as the paramedic swabbed the area with disinfectant and then probed for bullet fragments.

"Then please contact your personal physician before the day is out. He'll determine whether or not you need stitches, or just routine dressing changes until this heals. I don't think you've got any nerve damage, but he'll want to monitor you in order to be sure."

"Will do." Brian didn't admit that he was too new to the area to have found a doctor. He intended to rectify the situation on his own, though.

"The bullet's embedded in the floor," he said.

Glancing at him, Carrie paled.

"Remind me to tell the detective."

Brian scanned her facial features. Fragile and strong, that's what she is, he concluded as they stared at one another. He wondered again what had caused her to become so self-protective.

"Will you remind me?"

"Of course," she said.

Brian exhaled heavily when sterile gauze pads were applied to the wound, but other than moderate discomfort that he knew could be alleviated with aspirin, he felt fine.

Releasing Carrie's hand, he surged to his feet after the paramedic wrapped his upper arm with a length of gauze and taped it into place. A physically active man all of his life, Brian felt the need to walk off his tension and dispel the sense of confinement threatening to suffocate him.

He reminded himself that he still needed to give a preliminary statement to the police as he paced the carpeted area and tried to relax. He also kept a close watch on Carrie. He knew in his gut that she was just barely holding herself together.

As he stretched his legs Brian noticed that the paramedic appeared ready to shift his attention to her. He mentally saluted the man's thoroughness as he watched him pull on a fresh pair of surgical gloves.

"Miss?"

"Yes?"

"I'm going to check you out as well."

She shook her head. "There's no need, but thank you."

Brian intervened. As far as he was concerned, she looked on the verge of passing out. "She's not fine, but she's too stubborn to admit it."

Carrie flashed a frustrated look in his direction.

"Kind of like you?" remarked the paramedic as he looped a blood-pressure cuff around her upper arm. "Humor me, why don't you?" he encouraged his new patient.

She smiled faintly. "Were you a bulldozer in another life?"

The young man grinned as he positioned his stethoscope, then concentrated on the task at hand. "Good numbers considering the stress of the day. One-ten over seventy. Must be all that excercise," he said a minute later as he cast an appreciative glance at her unitard-clad body.

Detective Landis chose that moment to join them. Another man, also wearing a suit and carrying a notepad, accompanied him.

Brian shook hands with both men and gave them his name. Standing, Carrie did the same.

"Ms. Forbes, this is Field Agent Murphy of

the FBI. We'll be working together on this case, so he'll take your statement while I speak to Mr. York." Landis handed her the purse she'd dropped earlier. "One of the tellers said this was yours."

She nodded, accepting the leather shoulder bag and cradling it against her breasts.

Brian saw her white-knuckled hold on the bag. His concern for Carrie mounting, he moved to her side and placed his hand on her shoulder. "Are you sure you're all right?"

She shifted her stance, shrugging free of his touch. "Of course. I'm not . . . I'm just a little chilled right now."

Brian glanced at Landis. He could tell by the expression on the man's face that they were both thinking the same thing. She was experiencing a mild form of shock, understandable given the circumstances. The detective removed his suit jacket and draped it across her shoulders.

Carrie thanked him with a strained smile. Her chin lifted a notch as she looked at Brian.

He saw the control she exerted over herself, and he couldn't help admiring her innate strength and courage. It ate at him, though, that she'd pulled away from him.

"I appreciate what you did for me," she said quietly. "You saved my life, and saying thank you seems rather feeble, especially since you were shot because of me, but I don't really know what else to say right now."

"Carrie . . ."

"Don't forget about the bullet," she whispered before turning to Agent Murphy. "I'd like to give you my statement now, please."

Brian watched her walk away with the FBI agent. He told himself that he shouldn't care, but he did. He cared that she'd retreated from him. He cared that he probably wouldn't ever see her again. He cared about her, even though he hadn't wanted to care about anyone ever again.

Caring, he'd bitterly concluded at the time of his divorce a few years earlier, was nothing more than an invitation to failure.

An hour later Brian finally managed to do what he'd wanted to do since the robbery. He walked out of the bank and into the balmy warmth of the Southern California sunshine. Ignoring the shouted questions from the media and the curiosity seekers lined up on the sidewalk, he made his way around the side of the bank building and into the parking lot.

Pausing beside his car, he dug into his pocket for his keys, withdrew them, and promptly dropped them. Brian swore. He'd forgotten and used his injured arm. Pain had streaked like an arrow of flame all the way down his arm and into his hand when he'd attempted to insert the key in the lock.

"Why don't you let me drive you home?"

Brian turned at the sound of her voice.

Carrie bent down, rescued his car keys from the narrow strip of pavement that separated them, and straightened.

Brian's gaze fell on the keys cradled in the palm of her hand before shifting to her face. Her composure took him by surprise.

Looking up at him, she waited for him to respond.

"There's no need," he insisted, speaking far more sharply than he intended.

Carrie glanced at his bandaged arm. "There appears to be every need."

"Forget it."

"Then I guess I'll have to follow you."

"What in hell are you trying to prove?" he demanded, his temper much in evidence now.

"Absolutely nothing. You look as bad as I probably did a little while ago."

"You looked like death warmed over," Brian ground out.

"Thank you, kind sir."

He exhaled, the sound harsh. "Carrie . . ."

"Brian . . ." she singsonged right back at him.

He glared at her, then conceded, "You do look better now. Less like a piece of chalk."

"I get a little pale when my blusher fails me." She smiled. "Among my friends, I'm known for both my delayed reactions and my speedy recoveries."

"What else are you known for?" he asked. Her

smile faded, and he felt the sweep of her searching gaze as she studied him.

"I'm known for the fact that I am a very private person, but I suspect you're similarly inclined."

"Precisely, so put your mind at ease. I'm clear-headed enough to drive. Otherwise, I wouldn't attempt it. I'm also very tired and short-tempered enough right now to take the head off of anyone who crosses my path."

"A privacy freak and temperamental too," she mused.

He peered at her, his expression glacial again. "Your personality profile doesn't come as much of a surprise."

He heard a wealth of understanding and compassion in her mild tone of voice. Although he felt himself responding to her, he refused to relax his stance where she was concerned. He wanted her too much, and he sensed that the desire and need she inspired might be his downfall.

Brian extended his hand. "My keys, please."

Carrie deposited them in the palm of his outstretched hand. "I'm going to follow you in my car, so let's not have a debate, all right?"

The implacable expression on her face forced Brian to stop trying to dissuade her. "Have it your way."

"I intend to," she said as she walked to a late-model vehicle parked a few spaces away, got into it, and started the engine.

Brian saw her in his rearview mirror every time he glanced at it as she followed him down several tree-lined streets. When he pulled into the circular driveway in front of his newly constructed home, Carrie parked her car behind his.

Brian exited his vehicle, a sleek, top-of-the-line sports car designed by Detroit as a testament to the fantasies of every red-blooded male on the planet. He moved with a determined stride to the front door.

"Remarkable place," Carrie commented as she joined him.

Remarkable woman, he thought in response to her observation. He looked at her after inserting the key in the lock. This time he remembered to use his left hand.

"I've been wondering about the identity of the owner."

Shoving open the front door, Brian stepped to one side of it. "Now you know."

"Did you design the house yourself?"

"Tom Rainey handled it for me."

"I should have recognized his work. Several friends of mine have used his firm. He's very good." She smiled at him. "Your view of the Pacific must be amazing."

"It is," he agreed, captivated in spite of himself by the animation in her features and the pleasure sparkling in her hazel eyes.

The urge to touch her reignited with the force of a blowtorch within him. His jaw tightened, enhancing the angular lines of his face as he exercised ruthless self-control.

"We're neighbors," she said as she preceded him into the foyer of the contemporary dwelling. "I live a few blocks from here."

Brian dropped his keys atop one of several packing boxes stacked in the foyer, added his wallet and sunglasses to the pile, and then kicked off his deck shoes. He made his way to a leather chair positioned in front of a wall of windows in the living room.

Sinking down into the chair, he watched Carrie move slowly into the room. A breath shuddered free of his body as he took in the rich curves and inviting hollows poorly concealed by her athletic attire.

"It *is* amazing," Carrie confirmed, her delight resurfacing as she paused in the center of the room and took in the panoramic view that extended all the way to the horizon.

"I don't need a baby-sitter."

Glancing his way, she gently suggested, "Tell me something I haven't already figured out."

Brian shook his head, his expression growing stormy once again.

Setting her purse atop a coffee table, Carrie dropped to a crouch in front of him. "It's been a really tough day, the kind of day I wouldn't wish on my worst enemy. You helped me, and now I'm trying to help you." She paused for a moment, emotion filling her eyes.

He saw her fight for control, and he gripped the arms of his chair to keep himself from reaching for her and drawing her into his arms. He watched her force a smile back to her lips a few moments later.

"I don't want anything from you, Brian York, so relax. And for the record, I'm not the enemy."

"I never thought you were, but you've done your good deed for the month, so you can go now."

Carrie straightened, seemingly unperturbed by his irritability. "Before I leave, is there anyone I can call for you? A family member or a friend, perhaps."

"There's no one to call," he said in a flat voice.

Brian spoke the truth. He had no family to speak of, and other than a few business acquaintances, he'd kept his distance from people in the months since his arrival in California. That fact hadn't kept him from being invited to several A-list social functions already, but he rarely accepted those invitations, preferring instead to maintain his privacy.

Although he'd always kept a low profile, Brian York's entrepreneurial skills had made him something of a legend in the international business community. As a result, his professional peers and the media types who covered the world of high finance kept track of his comings and goings.

"All right, then." She worried her lip for a moment with her front teeth.

Brian tensed as he watched her. He thought of what it would be like to sample the taste and textures of her mouth. He felt his groin tighten, felt the desire that gushed into his veins and pummeled his entire body.

"Now what?" He knew his voice sounded raw, hungry, and he resented his response to her.

"Can I get you something to drink?"

"No."

"How about a clean shirt? The one you're wearing is . . ." Carrie hesitated, her gaze riveted on the bloodstains from his wound. "The one you're wearing is a total loss. If you'll tell me where your things are, I'll find you something else to wear."

If he let her do something constructive, he reasoned, then she'd leave, but when he spoke, he wasn't altogether certain if his motive was to hasten or delay her departure. "There's a sweatshirt on the end of my bed."

Carrie stood and stepped back.

Brian shoved himself to his feet. After tugging the tails of his shirt free of the waistband of his trousers, he started on the buttons with his left hand. His gaze remained fastened on Carrie the entire time.

She paled unexpectedly, then turned on her heel and headed for the hallway on the far side of the room. "I'll be right back."

"Last door on the right," he called after her.

Perplexed by her sudden skittishness, Brian

shrugged out of his shirt. An angry sound escaped him when the fabric pressed against his wounded upper arm. He wadded the bloodstained shirt into a ball and carried it into the kitchen, where he dropped it into the wastebasket.

Brian paused at the refrigerator, helped himself to a can of fruit juice, then returned to his chair in the living room. He downed the juice in two gulps, promised himself aspirin the next time he got up, and sank back in the soft leather. His eyes fell closed as he waited for Carrie, his thoughts mating with the images of her that filled his mind.

Carrie spotted the sweatshirt the instant she walked into the master suite, but her footsteps slowed to a stop before she reached the end of the bed. Brian's distinctive scent, that combination of citrusy aftershave and musky maleness that she'd noticed during their first moments together, whispered in the air.

She inhaled sharply, disconcerted by the wave of longing that washed over her, a longing for closeness never achieved.

Carrie chastised herself a moment later for indulging in wishful thinking. She reached for the sweatshirt. Holding the faded, much-laundered garment, she smoothed her fingertips across the fabric and glanced around the master suite.

The furniture, crafted in mahogany and very

masculine in style, still needed to be arranged in the room. Wardrobe boxes lined one wall. Smaller boxes, most still taped shut, had been stacked along another wall.

Exhaling softly, she sensed that Brian York was as much a loner as she'd become over the years. She couldn't help wondering why, although she doubted that she'd ever know the answer.

Forcing herself beyond her curiosity, Carrie returned to the living room. She found Brian seated once again in the chair, his head back and his eyes closed. Her gaze touched on the bandage circling his upper arm. Its whiteness contrasted with his sun-tinged skin, and it also reminded her that he'd put himself in harm's way because of her. His behavior, however instinctive, still amazed her. She functioned as an occasional rescuer in her work, but she couldn't recall a time when anyone had come to her assistance during a time of crisis.

She studied him then, tantalizing her senses as her eyes swept over his hard-featured face, lingered briefly on his sensually shaped mouth, and then moved on to his muscular chest. A dense pelt of black hair that started just above his pectorals in a pattern that reminded her of an inverted triangle swept down his powerful body to form a narrow line across a washboard-flat belly before disappearing from sight at the waistband of his trousers.

She felt her pulse pick up speed, felt a rush of something hot and wild flood her bloodstream. Sucking in a sharp breath, she told herself that she was behaving like a foolish adolescent, that wanting a man wasn't always enough.

Carrie shifted her gaze back to his face, suddenly realizing that he'd been watching her. Mortified that he'd caught her inspecting him like a side of beef at a meat market, she could tell by the tension in his hard jaw that he was none too pleased with her behavior.

"How are you feeling?" she asked, immediately embarrassed that she sounded so breathless.

He simply stared at her.

Dumb, dumb, dumb! she thought to herself. It's definitely time to leave.

"Brian?"

"Just great. Never been better."

She laughed, startled by his tone. "Sarcasm is your strong suit, isn't it?"

"So I've been told."

Carrie crossed the room. "I assume you'd prefer to do this yourself," she said as she handed him the sweatshirt.

He took the garment and dropped it onto the floor beside his chair. "You're very pale."

"Am I?" she asked, her gaze fixed on his face. She was determined to keep her eyes positioned well above the level of his broad shoulders.

"You are," he confirmed.

Carrie shrugged, trying to appear relaxed. "Given the morning we've just had, it's not surprising."

"There's a bottle of cognac on the kitchen counter. The snifters are in the cupboard above it."

She shook her head. "I don't drink."

"You'll find bottled water and fruit juices in the refrigerator."

"No, thank you."

"Are you always so well mannered?"

She smiled faintly. "Always."

"A lady."

"Yes," she answered, although she didn't feel ladylike at the moment.

"There really isn't any need for you to stay."

His abruptness made her step back. She knew she'd overstayed her welcome. She reached for her purse. "You're right."

"I know," he said quietly, his expression filled with a kind of weariness that Carrie recognized and understood.

Emotional fatigue. She told herself that the robbery had caused it in him, but some sixth sense and the bleakness in his eyes told her that Brian York was a complex man with a complicated history. Because her own past was something of a minefield, she didn't press him.

"I'm just a few blocks away, so if . . . if you need . . ." Her voice trailed off as his scrutiny of her intensified. Uncertainty made her shift uncomfortably.

"Why don't you give me your phone number?"

Genuinely surprised by his request, she nodded. "All right."

She suspected that he wouldn't call, even if he needed help. She knew in her heart that he was simply humoring her in order to facilitate her departure, because Brian York wasn't the kind of man who expressed need of any kind.

Is this a really good idea? a voice in her head inquired as she dug around in her purse for a business card that identified her as a crisis counselor. *Why don't you just ask him for his number and call periodically?* Carrie ignored the voice, wrote her home phone number on the back of the card, and placed it on the coffee table.

"Take care of yourself," Brian said.

"You too." Turning, she made her way out of the living room to the spacious foyer.

"Thank you."

Carrie paused in midstride, looked back over her shoulder, and whispered, "Thank *you.*"

She waited for a moment, but he said nothing more, so she let herself out of the house, locked the door behind her, and walked on shaking legs to her car.

Carrie sat in the driver's seat for several minutes before she managed to reclaim her composure, minutes during which her mind replayed the events that had taken place at the bank, minutes during which she faced the fact that a man she'd met under traumatic circumstances had awakened her sensuality and stirred her passions.

THREE

Carrie's blood ran like currents of ice through her veins as she studied the faces of the men assembled for the lineup. They stood in a row on the opposite side of a wall of one-way glass, staring straight ahead.

In the two days since the bank robbery, she'd begun to believe that she'd come to terms with the incident. Now, though, she knew she couldn't have been more wrong. Carrie trembled, recalling the violence that had brought Brian York into her life and forced her to confront her own mortality.

Although she hadn't heard from him, Brian rarely left her consciousness. Thoughts of him unsettled, aroused, and evoked curiosity and worry. He also prompted her to consider possibilities that she hadn't allowed herself to ponder in many years. Her final thought brought her up short.

Suddenly angry with herself for indulging in

such an inappropriate lapse, Carrie refocused on the men in the lineup and reminded herself of the serious nature of the task at hand. She wrapped her arms around her middle to ward off the chill settling over her as she stood beside Detective Landis in the small, semidark viewing room. Although she recognized one of the robbers, she took the time to inspect each individual in the lineup.

She quickly realized that the mental photo snapped in the first seconds of the robbery hadn't faded. Carrie now feared that it was permanently etched into her mind, just as another image from the past remained a part of her personal mental scrapbook. She'd made the wrong choice then, but she didn't intend to be guilty of that error in judgment this time.

"Number four," she said, glancing at Detective Landis after thoroughly scanning each man's face a second time.

"You're sure, Ms. Forbes?"

She nodded. "Very sure."

Landis took her arm and guided her out of the small room. "Will you testify?" he asked as they walked down the congested hallway at police headquarters.

Carrie responded without hesitation. "Of course."

The seasoned investigator gave her a measuring look. "You're certain?"

She paused. "I'm quite certain."

"Not everyone is so civic-minded."

"I don't feel civic-minded, Detective Landis. What I feel is anger and what I want is justice, but I know I have to help make it happen."

He nodded. "I understand what you're saying. I also know about your work at the Crisis Center. It would appear that you're willing to live the advice that you give to rape victims."

"I wouldn't have much credibility if I didn't, but that really isn't the point. This is personal. Very personal. If one or more of the robbers is prosecuted, I'm more than willing to participate as a witness."

He extended his hand. "Good enough. I'm grateful for your cooperation."

She smiled as they shook hands.

"We're building a very strong case against these guys," he assured her as they continued down the hallway. "The DA's office has assigned one of their best prosecutors."

Rounding a corner at the end of the hallway, Carrie spotted Brian. Her pulse raced as they joined him in the reception area.

"Mr. York identified the same man."

"I'm not surprised," Carrie managed to say.

"Landis, pick up line two," commanded a voice on the public-address system.

"Excuse me for a couple of minutes. I'll be right back," he assured Carrie and Brian. "Make yourselves comfortable." He waved in the direction of several chairs lined up against a wall in the reception area.

"We meet again," Carrie said once they were alone.

"But under improved circumstances. Did they call you in for the lineup?" he asked.

"Yes."

"Me too."

"Number four?"

"Number four," he clarified, the hard lines of his face looking etched in stone.

"How are you feeling?" she asked quietly.

"Good."

"I'm glad. Your arm doesn't seem to be bothering you," she observed as he collected a leather portfolio from a chair and held it with his right hand.

"It's healing. It's more an inconvenience than anything else."

Carrie nodded, although she remembered how much blood he'd lost and the pain he'd been in after being shot.

"How are you getting along?" Brian asked.

Carrie shrugged, still somewhat off balance by both the lineup and seeing Brian so unexpectedly. "All right." Sinking into the nearest chair, she set aside her purse and tried to control her response to him, but the effort proved futile.

Brian remained standing, his gaze direct and penetrating.

Carrie didn't know what to say.

"What's wrong?" he asked.

She looked away, forced once again to grapple with the longing she felt. "Nothing."

"You're lying."

Stung by his accusation, she reached for her purse.

"Don't leave. I was out of line just then, and I apologize."

She settled back in her chair, telling herself to calm down even as her temper flared. "You have the instincts of a drill instructor. Please refrain from using them on me. I don't like being called a liar."

"Point made and taken."

"Good."

Brian lowered himself into the chair beside hers. As she watched the fluid movement of his muscular body, Carrie thought of the safety she'd found in his encircling arms during the aftermath of the robbery. Desire flirted with her again, rousing her hunger for his touch. She inhaled sharply and chastised herself for having such reckless thoughts.

"Talk to me."

Blinking, she refocused on his face. "About what?"

"Anything."

"I think we've had this conversation before."

He nodded, his expression grim as he looked at her.

She sensed that his memories of the robbery

were still as vivid as her own. "I'm not feeling too chatty at the moment, Brian."

"I haven't called."

She frowned, not understanding the direction of his thoughts or his purpose in pointing out the obvious. "I know that."

"I've been busy."

"Unpacking?" she asked, her smile faint.

"That, and a few other things."

"Are you making much progress?" She felt utterly witless, asking him such mundane questions. She reminded herself that they were still strangers, in spite of the emotional intimacy that was a necessary consequence of having shared a life-changing event. "With the packing, I mean."

"Slow, but steady." Brian reached out as he spoke and took her hand.

Shocked by the contact, Carrie didn't resist when he wove his fingers through hers. She felt his warmth penetrate her skin and sink into her bones.

"I'm not—" Brian abruptly stopped speaking, his attention shifting beyond Carrie.

She turned and noticed Landis hurrying toward them. The look on his face hinted at a crisis. "Something's wrong," she said very softly to Brian.

"We've got a problem," Landis announced.

"Spell it out," Brian suggested as he released Carrie's hand and got to his feet.

"We lost one of the shooting victims. It happened about twenty minutes ago. This case is officially a robbery/homicide."

Carrie surged up from her chair, a murmur of distress escaping her. The memory of one of the paramedics crouched over a shooting victim as the man had been wheeled out of the bank lobby on a gurney slipped into the forefront of her mind.

She asked, "Was it the man who had a heart attack after he was shot?"

Landis nodded. "That's the one."

Brian slipped his arm around her shoulders.

Carrie welcomed the contact, welcomed his strength. She felt cold again. Very cold.

Landis, the tension he felt evident in his weathered face, studied them for a lingering moment. "Are you both still willing to testify?" he asked.

Carrie didn't hesitate. "Absolutely."

Brian nodded, but asked, "Is it necessary for Ms. Forbes to testify?"

Carrie wrenched free of him, shocked by his question and poised to protest his high-handedness.

"Wait, please," he responded.

Landis exhaled heavily. "Other than you two and a third person who's likely to back out on us when push comes to shove, no one else is willing."

"No one?" Incredulity underscored Brian's question. "There had to be at least a dozen people in that place during the robbery, and nobody's willing to step forward?"

Landis shook his head. "Someone leaked information to the press, and the priors on our perps are now public knowledge. They're also suspects in three other bank jobs. Look, I won't try to kid you. These guys are really bad news. Everyone's running scared except you two."

"You have us both," Carrie interjected, no longer willing or able to remain silent.

"Thank you, Ms. Forbes."

"Two of the men are still at large, Landis," Brian reminded him.

"We're close to nailing them."

"How close?" he asked.

"We almost had them a few hours ago."

"What happened?"

"What always happens when you're dealing with violent career criminals. They're on the move, and they're willing to take down anyone who gets in their way. One of the officers who spotted them this morning and attempted to take them into custody is in surgery."

Alarmed by the news, Carrie asked, "Will he survive?"

"His prognosis is excellent."

Brian swore.

She flinched at the angry word, but her conviction that she had to testify intensified. "What do we do next?"

"The district attorney's office will want to follow up on your signed statements with interviews."

"When?" Brian asked.

"Fairly soon, I would imagine."

"You have both of my phone numbers." Carrie shot a warning glance at Brian before she continued. "I'm not changing my mind, Detective. I have every intention of testifying."

Her position unequivocally stated, Carrie reclaimed her purse and walked away. She stepped onto a crowded elevator across from the reception area as soon as the doors opened.

Brian's eyes narrowed when he noticed the person who boarded the elevator right after Carrie. What appeared to be a bulky camera bag was slung over the lanky man's shoulder. As he turned to face forward Brian saw the press badge pinned to his jacket. The elevator doors closed before he could point the man out to Landis.

"She's quite a lady," Landis remarked.

He nodded, momentarily distracted from the worry nibbling at the edge of his mind. "I still don't want her placed in a vulnerable position if it can be avoided."

The detective chuckled. "She didn't appreciate your protective instincts at all, did she?"

Brian spoke with his usual bluntness. "She means well, but I'm sure you've already figured out that some people in this world don't always weigh the long-term consequences of the choices they make."

Landis shrugged. "You're right, of course, but Carrie Forbes is one determined woman, and I need her to help make this case. I won't try to talk her out of testifying. I can't."

Frustrated with the situation and the potential jeopardy to Carrie, Brian conceded, "I've figured that out."

"It's time for me to get back to the salt mines," Landis said.

"Keep me posted on your progress," Brian urged as the two men shook hands.

"Will do, Mr. York."

Brian bypassed the elevator in favor of using the stairs. Making his way out of police headquarters, he entered the parking garage. He spotted Carrie as he walked to his car. Head bowed, she stood by the open door of her vehicle.

As he approached her Brian saw the tremors passing through her slender body and her white-knuckled grip on the door frame. He responded instinctively to her obvious need. He didn't question the impulse.

"Another one of your famous delayed reactions?" he asked in a subdued voice as he paused behind her.

Carrie nodded, but she didn't turn around.

Brian slid his arms around her waist and gently drew her back against his body.

Still trembling, she stiffened at his touch.

He didn't release her, despite the fact that she felt rigid enough beneath his hands to shatter if subjected to even the slightest pressure. "Let your feelings out before they choke you," Brian advised.

He felt the shudder that passed through her, then the slow easing of tension in her body. Lowering his head, he gathered her close and pressed his cheek against the side of her face. He closed his eyes then and savored the feel of her. The mingling scents of vanilla and spice that emanated from her skin filled his senses.

Intent on offering her reassurance and comfort, he realized that he derived those things and more from her. The realization shocked him and forced him to confront the barrenness of his own life in recent years.

Carrie shifted suddenly, turning in the circle of his arms. "Why do you care?" she asked, tears sparkling like jewels on her lower lashes as she looked up at him.

Brian stared at her heart-shaped face. He felt in danger of drowning in the depths of her densely lashed hazel eyes. He felt, as well, the fist of desire that closed around his heart, its grip so fierce that shock reverberated within him.

Why do you care? she'd asked.

How could he not care? Brian wondered in a moment of stark honesty with himself as his gaze fell to the richly sensual shape of her lips, lips that he wanted to taste, then linger over until she granted him permission to delve beyond and explore what he sensed would be the honeyed recesses of her mouth.

Instead of speaking, Brian shook his head and kept his arms around her. Carrie shuddered, then leaned into him, her full breasts plumping against his chest, her hips fitting to his loins like interlocking puzzle pieces. He promised himself that he would offer nothing more than comfort and compassion, but his body made a liar out of him as it exploded with response to their intimate alignment. Heat streaked into his bloodstream.

Brian York fought a battle for control in the minutes that followed, but his desire for Carrie made a mockery of his efforts to contain his reaction to her. The muscles of his body tremored perceptibly, and his hold on her tightened. He drew in a harsh breath.

Lifting her head from his shoulder, Carrie stared at him. She opened her mouth to speak, but closed it as if defeated suddenly by her awareness of what was happening to him.

Before she lowered her gaze, he glimpsed an array of emotions in her expressive features. Shock. Disbelief. Hunger. Fear. Anguish.

Looking at her was like peering into his own soul. Stunned, Brian dug his fingers into her waist. Although he wanted her, wanted to sink into her flesh and brand it with the heat of his desire, he managed to hold back.

A tear slipped down her cheek.

His desire retreated like a thief in the night. Regret and concern replaced it. He sensed then that she was grappling with far more than the lineup and the revelation that one of the bank patrons had died.

She dragged in a strangled breath, then exhaled. "I'm sorry."

"Don't apologize."

"Why not?" She pushed at the tendrils of auburn hair that had fallen across her cheek. "I'm falling apart, and I feel like an idiot right now."

"Stress does that to a person. You don't have to testify, Carrie."

"Yes, I do," she insisted, trying to ease free of him.

"For all the wrong reasons."

She shook her head. Determination glittered in her eyes. "No. For the right reasons."

"This time?" he speculated, firing a shot in the dark.

Surprise widened her eyes.

Bull's-eye!

She gave him a wary look.

He felt the stillness that settled over her. "Tell me about your reasons," he encouraged.

"My reasons don't concern you, Brian."

"Make an exception," he urged, sensing that it was important for her to talk. "You're all bottled up inside, and I'm willing to be your sounding board."

She straightened, squaring her shoulders as she looked directly at him. "You're intruding on my personal life. Look, I really do know what I'm doing, but thank you for offering."

Her boundary lines were in place again, Brian realized. "It's open-ended."

"We don't know each other well enough for me to . . ." Her voice trailed off.

"And you're a very private person," he finished for her.

"I don't want to talk about why. Just accept that I'm going to testify. No one, not even you, can stop me. So don't bother to try."

"Is this some kind of penance for a mistake you made a long time ago?" he pressed.

She tried to step back.

"Don't," he said, unwilling to release her.

"You're prying," she accused, her hands fisted at her sides as she stared at his chest.

"I feel like I have to, even though I don't know why."

"I won't change my mind."

He nodded, believing her. "Carrie?" he said quietly.

She lifted her face, eyes wide and skin so pale, it gave her an ethereal look.

Brian felt something shatter inside himself. Restraint, he decided as he lowered his head. Guided solely by instinct in the moments that followed, he claimed her mouth. He told himself that they both needed the connection, that they both craved the closeness he'd just initiated. His conscience called him a liar, but he ignored it. He couldn't do anything else.

She stood stiffly in the circle of his arms, still

enough to remind him of a living statue, until air suddenly gushed past her lips and her entire body softened.

The desire he felt for her pounded through his veins with the fury and force of a sledgehammer.

Bringing his hands up to frame her face, he brushed his lips back and forth across hers in a tender assault. He felt the trembling of her entire body. Hungry enough to risk her rejection, he traced the width of her lower lip with the tip of his tongue.

Carrie clutched at the front of his shirt, her fingers digging into the fabric. Seconds later she hesitantly parted her lips, angled her head, and granted him the access he sought.

Brian groaned.

She felt encompassed by the sound.

He explored her with infinite tenderness.

Carrie tasted his desire as their mouths fused. Shock rocked her. Acute hunger overwhelmed her, making her feel as though an army had successfully breached the walls of her heart and would soon conquer her soul.

She surrendered to Brian's desire and to her own, although for a fleeting moment she questioned his motives. But his gentleness seduced her, seduced her so thoroughly that she stopped thinking and willingly sank into the pool of erotic sensations that submerged any resistance she might have thought to muster.

He kissed her deeply, thoroughly, but with

care and a kind of gentleness that she'd never known before. She nearly wept as she responded to him with a desire that she'd never expected to feel for anyone, thanks to a past that had muted her emotions.

Carrie allowed him to sweep away her awareness of everything but him. She focused on the firmness of his lips, the minty flavor of his mouth, the heat generated by his strong body, and the sensations swirling around inside her.

She welcomed his tongue when it darted into her mouth. She embraced the intimate intrusion, although it brought with it feelings she'd feared in the past, feelings utterly foreign to a woman who thought she'd adjusted to a life spent on the sidelines. Watching others share laughter and love, joy and sorrow, failure and triumphs. Watching others experiencing what she'd dreamed of for herself.

Carrie lifted her arms and tangled her fingers at his nape, molding herself to Brian, savoring his physical strength, basking in the exploration he conducted with his mouth and hands. Currents of desire flowed in her veins, melting the ice that had formed within her during the time she had viewed the lineup.

He alternately sipped from her lips and invaded her mouth, his body becoming so hard that it felt like carved stone beneath her fingers.

A car horn suddenly blared, startling them both.

Carrie jerked free of Brian, disoriented as she looked around the crowded parking garage for the source of the sound. Another impatient driver pounded on his car horn in short, angry bleats that brought to mind what she'd thought were firecrackers at the bank. For an instant she was transported back to the first moments of the robbery. A cry of disbelief escaped her.

Brian reached for her and caught her hand before she could duck into her car.

"It's all right," he insisted.

Carrie slowly nodded, her panic subsiding. Still, her heart raced wildly beneath her breasts.

They stared at each other then, both breathing like winded marathoners, both clearly thinking of what they'd just shared.

Carrie saw in Brian's features what she herself had felt as he'd touched her and kissed her. Desire. Pure, stark desire that still flared in his dark eyes and tightened the already hard angles of his face.

Her gaze riveted on him as she searched for a way to reclaim her poise, she didn't notice the man shielded from view by a delivery van—the man who shot a series of photographs and then disappeared into the shadows before anyone spotted him.

"We . . ." Carrie began, still reeling from the intimacy they'd shared.

". . . shouldn't?" he finished for her.

She nodded, appalled by her own behavior and

stunned by the desire still flowing through her body.

"It's the situation we're in," he said.

"Is it?" Her voice was faint.

"It's part of it."

She pressed the fingertips of her free hand to her forehead. "I feel like an idiot."

He tightened his grip on her wrist. "There's no need."

"Let go of me, please."

He did. Instantly.

"I apologize," she said.

"For what?" he asked. "I needed you as much as you needed me."

"I hate falling apart every five seconds."

"You hate losing control," he countered. "There's a difference."

She exhaled. "True."

"Why does it bother you so much to lean on me?"

Flushing, she turned away and dug her keys out of her purse.

"Running away isn't your style any longer," he reminded her.

She bowed her head, trying again to gather up the loose threads of her dignity.

"Carrie?"

"What?"

"Don't be embarrassed. That was just simple need. It happens to everyone at one time or another."

She didn't say anything as she got into her car and secured her seat belt. She couldn't. She'd written the textbook on need—correction, *unfulfilled* need.

Brian leaned down. "Look at me."

She did, but very reluctantly.

"You're a remarkable woman, Carrie Forbes."

She searched his face, wanting to believe him but knowing the truth about herself. She felt like a coward most of the time. "You're being kind."

"I've never been accused of kindness."

"You're more kind than you know."

"I didn't kiss you because I was feeling kind."

She searched his face, her gaze finally snagging on his dark eyes. "Then why?"

"I'm not sure." He straightened and stepped back from her car. "That's not true. I do know."

"Tell me," she whispered.

"I needed your warmth. I needed you."

Carrie stared at him, shocked by his admission because it accurately mirrored the feelings she didn't possess the courage to acknowledge.

"Take care of yourself," she said before turning the ignition key and backing her car out of the parking space.

Just before she guided the car around a corner and exited the parking lot, she caught a final glimpse of Brian York. His image, and the memory of his touch and taste, stayed with her for the rest of the day.

FOUR

"Carrie Forbes."

She froze for a moment, certain that she'd heard the distinctive sound of Brian York's voice. Not possible, she decided. Her brain had taken a leave of absence, she told herself.

"It would seem that it's our destiny to keep running into each other."

He wasn't a figment of her imagination, Carrie realized as she turned to greet him in her capacity as a board member doing her duty in the receiving line at the annual fund-raiser. She made herself smile, made herself meet Brian's steady gaze as she extended her hand.

"Welcome to the Crisis Center fund-raiser."

"Surprised?" he asked, smiling back at her as he clasped her hand in a firm grip.

She started to tremble inside as she felt the

warmth of his skin invade her fingers. "You know I am, but that was your intent, wasn't it?"

Her gaze dipped to his chest, and she noted the badge he wore, a color-coded name tag that indicated his status as a generous donator to a volunteer organization dedicated to the needs of sexual-assault victims. She didn't take the time to question his invitation to the gala fund-raiser, because she knew from experience that the fund-raising staff routinely included on the guest list the most powerful and influential of the monied elite who called the Southern California coast home.

"I almost called you."

"But you didn't," she pointed out.

He shook his head. "Forgive me?"

Carrie saw that he wasn't even remotely penitent, but she played his game nonetheless. "Of course."

He grinned then, as if to make it clear that he didn't believe her.

Although her face ached from the effort required to keep her smile in place, she managed the task as she spoke. "I hope you enjoy the evening. The chef from La Valencia in La Jolla designed our menu, and the orchestra has an excellent reputation."

"That was very well done," he remarked in a quiet voice not meant to be overheard. "Polite, but effectively dismissive."

Carrie stiffened, then attempted to withdraw her hand.

Brian refused to cooperate. "Do I need to remind you that I'm not a threat?"

"This is hardly the time or—"

"—or the place," he finished for her, his dark eyes sweeping over her and then lingering on her lips.

She suddenly felt warm all over. "What are you trying to prove?" she demanded.

He shook his head. "Not a thing."

Carrie saw an odd mixture of laughter and seriousness in his face. "I don't believe you."

He chuckled. "You probably shouldn't, now that I think about it."

"Brian . . ." she began.

The humor in his expression disappeared. "I like the way my name sounds when you say it."

Carrie pressed her fingertips to her forehead, flustered by this man and the temptation he posed. She remembered the feel of his hands on her body, the strength he'd leashed as he'd held her, and the seductive way he'd kissed her. She nearly moaned, but she managed to contain herself and her response to his impact on her senses.

Damn him! she thought. Why is he doing this to me?

"Carrie?"

She blinked and refocused on him. "What?"

"You look exquisite."

"Thank you," she whispered, shocked to discover that his opinion mattered.

Several friends at the center knew about her experience during the bank robbery, and some had suggested that she not bother to attend the fund-raiser. As a result, she'd gone to great effort to prepare for the evening, her determination to appear unaffected by the events of the previous few days fueling the attention she'd given to her attire, upswept hairstyle, and makeup.

"Dance with me later?"

She couldn't let him touch her again, Carrie realized as she watched him with a wary expression and worried her lower lip with her teeth.

"It's a shame that we're not alone right now," he said very softly.

She frowned at him before glancing to her left. The other board members were dispersing. She suspected that Brian had deliberately timed his arrival so that he wouldn't be rushed through the receiving line.

He stepped closer. "It really is a shame."

Carrie moved backward, feeling like a pawn on a chessboard. The wall behind her halted her retreat. She ground her jaws together in frustration.

"Don't you want to know why?"

His proximity and his height forced her to tilt her head in order to keep her eyes on his face. "Why?" she asked, although she doubted she'd like his answer.

"Because I'd like to kiss you again," he said bluntly.

She knew it! She hated his answer. *Liar*, her conscience screeched. "How did you know I'd be here?"

"It wasn't too tough to figure out. Your business card, an invitation to a fund-raiser in a stack of mail I finally got around to opening this afternoon, a phone call to a friend, a few questions." He shrugged, his broad shoulders shifting powerfully beneath his custom-fitted dinner jacket. "You get the picture, I'm sure."

She jerked her hand free. "You should be working for Detective Landis."

He grinned. "So, will you dance with me?"

Carrie smiled, but the expression on her face contained all the warmth of an arctic weather front. "If my duties don't keep me off the dance floor."

Brian sobered, his gaze sweeping over her once more. Lifting his hand, he touched her cheek with his fingertips. He frowned as he traced the side of her face.

Staring up at him, Carrie unconsciously held her breath.

Brian slowly withdrew his hand.

She exhaled in a gush of air.

"Don't be afraid of me, please."

You terrify me! she thought. You make me crave things I can't have, will never have.

She stared at him, stunned by his intense expression, his comment, and the gentleness of his caress. "Brian . . . I can't . . ." risk getting involved with you, she nearly said, but she managed to stop herself in time. Sounding like a fool wasn't on her list of things to do that night.

He shook his head. "One dance, Carrie. Just one. I need your warmth." Abruptly turning, he walked away.

Dumbstruck, she watched him disappear into the crowd of attendees currently converging on the entrance to the ballroom.

"The speakers are almost ready to begin, Carrie. We should take our seats now."

She nodded absently.

"Are you ill, my dear?" asked Elizabeth Morton, an attractive silver-haired matron and one of the original founders of the Crisis Center. "If you don't feel well enough to . . ."

That snapped her back to the present. No one, not even Brian York, she vowed, would be allowed to distract her from the purpose of the evening. The strained coffers of the center needed every donated dollar the board could attract from its patrons if it was to survive. And she was dedicated to the survival of the Crisis Center.

Squaring her shoulders, she smoothed a shaking hand over the midriff of her intricately beaded gown. "I'm fine, Elizabeth."

"You don't look fine."

Carrie forced a smile to her lips as she linked arms with her fellow board member and longtime friend. "Let's take our seats, shall we? Howard hates it when you disappear on him."

Elizabeth Morton laughed softly as they entered the crowded ballroom. "You'd think after forty years of marriage he'd be less possessive."

Carrie glanced at the woman. "You know you love it, Elizabeth. I suspect you'd divorce him if he weren't so attentive."

"You're probably right," Elizabeth conceded, then continued primly, "Our children would be quite shocked."

Along with Elizabeth, Carrie took her seat at the table reserved for the board members and their spouses. As she observed each of the couples at the circular table, she couldn't help reflecting on the emptiness of her own life in the years since her broken engagement. She envied these couples the relaxed banter they shared, envied the exchanged looks of understanding, the spontaneous gestures of affection.

They were emotionally intimate, Carrie realized. She wondered if they grasped the gift they'd been given in their relationships.

She sighed, suddenly annoyed with herself for falling into such a melancholy mood. She pasted a pleasant expression on her face and tried to cast Brian York from her thoughts. She failed miserably, in large part thanks to the fact that he was seated within view.

Each time she looked up from her plate, she caught him studying her. His enigmatic expression made it impossible for her to discern his thoughts, but that didn't prevent her from trying to understand his motives. Another useless endeavor, she finally concluded when he lifted his wineglass in a silent toast as he returned her gaze.

She refused to run, though, refused to be driven from her responsibilities to the center. Although she picked at her food as the speakers took their turns at the podium, she roused herself to join in the enthusiastic applause when it was announced that the center had exceeded the goal established for donations. The budget for the next year now assured, Carrie breathed an internal sigh of relief.

In her capacity as one of the senior counselors, Carrie was introduced by the master of ceremonies in order to provide the attendees with an overview of the extensive medical, psychological, and legal services available at the Crisis Center. Waiters quietly circulated among the tables, pouring coffee, serving pastries, and taking orders for after-dinner liquers during her presentation.

She felt the press of Brian's gaze as she spoke. Although she repeatedly made eye contact with several audience members, she managed not to look at him. Gathering up her notes and leaving the podium once she completed her remarks, she decided to excuse herself from the fund-raiser before the orchestra started to play. She intended to plead fatigue if anyone questioned her departure, then make a fast getaway.

She hated running, but she hated feeling trapped even more. And Brian York, for all his undeniable appeal, represented a trap, one that could easily be triggered by the desire she felt to experience his embrace once more.

Carrie hesitated when she saw Brian standing beside the short staircase that led to the stage, his hand extended to assist her so that she could navigate the steps in her long gown. She knew she couldn't ignore him. Rudeness didn't suit her. Neither did drawing attention to herself, which she suspected would happen if she misstepped and landed on her nose.

"You're about to run for the nearest exit, aren't you?"

She withdrew her hand as she paused beside him at the bottom of the staircase. She couldn't deny the obvious. "I was giving the notion some very serious consideration."

"I thought so."

"I've had a long day, Brian."

He nodded, his expression somber. "I understand."

She exhaled softly. Why, she wondered, did he have to be kind when she least expected it?

He took her arm, guiding her back to the now-empty table that she'd shared with the other board members, but he didn't say anything.

Carrie shifted uneasily as she returned his gaze. Desire that reminded her of a blast of steam heat invaded her bloodstream, and she visibly trembled.

"Don't run from me, Carrie."

I should, she thought, *but I can't seem to make my legs work.* "I'm not," she whispered.

"Aren't you about to?"

"Brian, this is crazy. We don't really know each other."

"We can change that."

Still immobilized by the desire she felt, she reminded herself of reality. *Her* reality.

Behind them, members of the orchestra moved onto the stage. Several musicians tested their instruments. Carrie absently registered the various sounds.

"Dance with me?"

She picked up her beaded evening purse, clutching it so tightly that her fingers started to throb. "There's no music."

"There will be in a few minutes."

She peered up at him, only vaguely aware of the milling crowd and laughter-filled conversations taking place around them. Hotel employees began shifting tables in order to expand the circumference of the ballroom dance floor.

"We're in the way," he said as two men removed the chairs circling the table.

She nodded, but the words he'd spoken didn't really register until he took her free hand and led her to an alcove on the perimeter of the ballroom. Glancing over her shoulder, Carrie finally noticed the curious glances being directed their way by several of her acquaintances. She turned, positioning herself so that her back was to the crowd, and drew in a steadying breath.

"I'm starting to get the impression that the prospect of dancing with me ranks right up there in your mind with cruel and unusual punishment."

Carrie shook her head, denial instinctive. "It's not that, Brian."

"Then what's bothering you?"

She exhaled, lifted her chin, and said honestly, "You make me nervous."

"Because I want you?"

She knew his bluntness shouldn't have startled her. It was typically Brian York. Carrie didn't shy away from his question or his bold gaze. "Yes," she answered with equal candor, acknowledging his interest in her.

He smiled, his expression faintly ironic. "You make me just as nervous."

She gave him a skeptical look. "I doubt that."

"Don't. It's the truth."

"Then we would be wise not to tempt fate, wouldn't we? And we would be wiser still if we didn't make mistakes in judgment simply because we shared a difficult experience?"

"Where is the wisdom in ignoring mutual need in the aftermath of a tragedy?" he asked.

"Stress can be dealt with in a variety of ways."

"Perhaps, but I'm not talking about stress. I'm talking about need."

"You can't separate the two," Carrie insisted. "Not in this situation, anyway."

"Are you afraid of being used?"

"Of course. Who isn't?"

Brian hesitated, then said, "I wouldn't do that to you. Treating a woman like a Band-Aid isn't my style."

"I don't think you'd do it on purpose, but the possibility exists, however unintentional."

His gaze narrowed. "You're afraid of more than being used."

She stiffened. "I'm thirty-five, Brian, not fifteen. I have baggage from the past, just like every other adult in this ballroom. I'm not unique."

"I disagree. I think you're quite unique, Carrie Forbes. In fact, you're probably the most unique woman I've ever met."

She stared at him. "You sound angry."

He shoved ruthless fingers through the dense dark hair that capped his head. "I'm not angry."

The orchestra began to play, as though to punctuate his remark. Carrie felt compassion rise up within her like a tidal wave as she studied his expressive eyes. The pain she'd glimpsed in him at the bank had returned, but this time it reminded her of some of the disillusionment she'd experienced in her own life.

She felt the barriers surrounding her heart start to give way, tumbling free like a house of cards subjected to a gusting wind. She sensed the utter futility of denying herself the pleasure of standing within the circle of his arms once more. She also acknowledged the yearning within her heart to feel emotionally connected to Brian, if only for a short while.

He needed her.

She needed him.

Need.

It seemed simple, but it was oh so complicated.

Carrie consciously accepted the risk of the choice she was about to make. She refused to be guided by her fear of either the known or unknown any longer. The risk of caring too much for Brian was a reality she knew she had to confront, but first she wanted one more chance to imprint her senses with his touch, his masculine scent, and perhaps even indulge herself with one last taste of him.

Desire coiled tightly within her, making her tremble all over. Carrie wanted to feel again. She wanted, she realized, so much, but she knew better than to indulge in greed. A piece of the pie would have to suffice. Afterward, she knew she would have to deal with the hunger that remained.

After positioning the strap of her beaded purse over her shoulder, Carrie pressed her hands together, exhaled shakily, then said, "I like you and I'm attracted to you, but I know my own limits as a person, so I'm asking you to respect my feelings. Will you do that for me?"

He nodded. "The rules are up to you."

"Then I'll dance with you," she whispered.

Brian discovered that it was his turn to be shocked. He didn't question his good fortune, though. He silently led Carrie back to the dance floor. As he drew her into his arms he experienced a sense of relief that was unlike anything he'd ever known before.

She looked up at him. "I'm a little out of practice, so I'll apologize in advance for stepping on your toes."

Brian smiled. "You're no more out of practice than your partner. I guess we'll have to wing it."

"You're being kind again," she observed.

"I think I told you I'm not known for my kindness."

Her expression grew serious. "You're many things, Brian York, and kind is one of them."

Amazed by her perception of him, he held her close as they moved around the dance floor. The orchestra cooperated with his need to have her in his arms by playing a series of waltzes. They danced together in silence and with the kind of fluid physical harmony normally evident only with longtime lovers.

Brian sensed then that making love to her would be the ultimate pleasure. He savored the hourglass shape of Carrie's body, and he breathed in the subtle scent of spiced vanilla he knew he would always connect to her. He managed, at first and by the sheer force of his will, to keep the desire he felt for her at bay, aware that the threat of it spiraling beyond his control was just a heartbeat away.

But each time she brushed against him, each time he felt the shape of her full, firm breasts against his chest or the feminine width of her hips shifting against his loins, he also felt his temperature rise and his pulse accelerate. His hunger for her finally sent heat spewing into his bloodstream and made the muscles in his body tighten with an elemental kind of desire he hadn't experienced in many years.

He also felt the fine trembling that whispered through her body, heard the sighs that escaped her. Even her skin felt hot to the touch. Experienced enough to recognize Carrie's arousal for what it was, Brian also recognized her uneasiness with her response to him.

He didn't press her, even though he wanted to bury himself in her sensual heat. He longed to lose himself in her depths, and he longed to feel the cleansing, simmering rain of her sensuality. Instead of revealing his hunger, however, he simply held her, in spite of the currents of desire forging a scorching path of response through his veins.

Brian couldn't recall a time in his life when he'd wanted a woman more than he wanted Carrie. Sensitive and complex, she challenged him. He didn't view her as a conquest, though. As they danced he grappled with the self-protective urge to compartmentalize her, to explain away the chemistry that taunted him as a natural result of her understated beauty, his loner lifestyle in recent years, and the trauma of the bank robbery. He failed, however. His innate honesty and his instincts forced him to acknowledge the reality that he wanted much more from her than sexual gratification. He had little to give in return. He knew that fact as well as he knew his own name, because it had been pointed out to him repeatedly.

Still, he craved her gentleness, her tender nature, and her compassion—almost as much as he craved her passion, which simmered just below her elegant surface. Carrie possessed an innate sensuality that spoke to him. It tempted him as well, tempted him to ignore the painful lessons of his past in favor of exploring a relationship with her.

But ringing in his ears were the accusations of neglect and indifference his ex-wife had made near the end of their marriage, accusations that echoed within his soul and made him doubt himself during those lonely moments when he let himself dwell on his failure as a husband and a partner.

He'd emerged from his divorce convinced that he lacked the ability to sustain a loving relationship. He believed himself to be deficient. As a result, his conscience cautioned him against creating expectations that he would never be able to realize, cautioned him not to tamper with the emotions of the woman in his arms, the same woman who aroused his passions to a fever pitch, but who also provoked within him the need to protect her from both his failings and his hunger.

"You're awfully quiet," Carrie observed.

Brian glanced down at her. "Just enjoying the moment and the woman in my arms."

She smiled hesitantly. "Me too."

Gathering her into his heat and strength, he lowered his head and pressed a kiss to her forehead.

She trembled, apprehension shadowing her hazel eyes as her smile faded. "What was that for?"

He felt his loins tighten with even greater tension. "To thank you."

"For what?"

"For sharing your warmth."

Tears filled her eyes. "I didn't expect you, Brian York."

Her emotional nakedness startled him. "I know what you mean," he finally said, because he did.

FIVE

The door chimes jarred Carrie out of a sound sleep the next morning. A glance at the clock on her bedside table told her that it was only a few minutes after six.

"Go away," she muttered as she tugged the sheet over her head. To her frustration, the sound of peeling chimes persisted.

Groaning, Carrie shoved aside the covers and reached for her bathrobe. The chimes continued to echo through the house as she walked the length of the hallway and approached the front door.

Although still half-asleep, she had the presence of mind to peer through the peephole before jerking open the heavy oak door. The shock of finding Brian on her doorstep stilled the harsh words that were about to spill past her lips.

She immediately noticed the stormy expression on his face. "What's wrong?"

"Did I wake you?"

Carrie shoved at the lock of auburn hair that had fallen into her eyes. She hated facing anyone without a scrubbed face and brushed teeth.

"Yes, you woke me," she admitted, good manners consigned to a more rational hour.

"May I come in?"

"Why? I mean . . ."

"It's important, Carrie. I wouldn't be here otherwise."

Searching his face, she saw his sincerity. She motioned him inside and then closed the front door after him.

"I need coffee," she announced as she stumbled barefoot in the direction of the kitchen.

"Good idea." He followed her down the hallway and into the first room in the house to receive the morning sun each day.

Carrie said a prayer of thanks when she noticed the already full coffeepot, courtesy of the timer she routinely used. Reaching for two mugs from the cupboard nearest the coffeemaker, she kept her back to Brian, mourned the fact that she'd had only four hours of sleep as she poured their coffee, and then turned to face him.

"Cream? Sugar?" she asked in the verbal shorthand reserved for unexpected guests who showed up at ungodly hours.

"Black, please."

She nodded and handed him one of the mugs. She took a healthy taste of the steaming brew from her own mug before speaking again. "What's wrong?"

"We've got a major problem."

The man has a talent for understatement, she decided. "That's obvious."

"I didn't want to discuss this with you on the phone."

She studied him, awake enough now to notice the snug fit of faded jeans over his powerful thighs and the shirt that did nothing to conceal the muscular width of his chest. The man was too virile for her mental health. He hadn't shaved, she realized as her gaze swept over his strong jaw. She sighed, then took another sip of coffee.

"Carrie?"

She blinked, then noticed his amused expression. "Yes?"

"Are you always like this in the morning?"

"Like what?"

"Disconnected. Dreamy."

She might have smiled if her senses hadn't been in such disarray. She still hadn't come to terms with the effect he had on her, and she wondered if she ever would. He'd strolled in and out of her subconscious mind while she'd slept. She'd awakened repeatedly, feeling tortured by the arousal that moved hotly, sluggishly through her entire body. Even now, she felt hungry for his touch and the taste of him. Especially now, she realized with alarm.

"Earth to Carrie."

Exhaling raggedly, she pulled herself together enough to respond to his observation. "I don't usually start my day at a fast gallop when I've only had a few hours of sleep. I like to ease into it very slowly."

Brian conceded, "I don't rush the process either, under normal conditions."

She sobered, aware that they could have easily been talking about something else altogether, something that tempted them both, something that she felt compelled to prevent. She watched him then and waited for him to speak.

He watched her in return, the tension she'd noticed in his expression and posture when he'd faced her at the front door returning tenfold. Something was wrong, Carrie reminded herself as she set aside her conflicted emotions and concentrated on Brian's demeanor. Very wrong.

"I'm listening," she encouraged.

"Today's different."

"I gathered that." She noticed the newspaper clutched in his left hand and gave him an expectant look.

Brian walked to the kitchen table and spread the paper out atop it. "Take a look," he ordered, his tone harsh.

That woke her up more than anything. She loathed being ordered around by anyone.

"The drill instructor's back," she remarked, stubborn enough not to budge from her slouched position against the edge of the counter despite her growing curiosity. She took another sip of coffee and returned his gaze.

"Take a look . . . please."

"Put that way . . ." Carrie crossed the kitchen and glanced down at the front page. The pleasant expression on her face and most of the sleep-induced flush of her complexion disappeared. "My God!"

Brian uttered a sharp word, a concise expletive that punctuated her outburst, contained utter fury, and might even have annoyed her under other circumstances.

Horrified, she exclaimed, "I don't believe this!"

"Believe it," he advised grimly.

"How could anyone be so stupid?"

"Some people don't care what they have to do when they're intent on making a fast buck."

"But to expose us this way."

"Journalistic excellence," he said sarcastically.

"We were followed after the lineup."

He nodded.

"They—"

"—or he . . ." Brian supplied.

Shock briefly silenced her as Carrie stared disbelievingly at the newspaper's front page.

"—saw us in the parking garage," she finished on a gush of pent-up air a few moments later.

Brian jerked a nod in her direction.

Still stunned by the invasion of their privacy, Carrie studied the grainy photo and the headline atop it as she set aside her coffee mug. The headline WITNESSES TO BANK ROBBERY/HOMICIDE TO TESTIFY seemed to jump off the page and smack her in the face.

A chill moved through her, then settled into her bones. As she studied the picture of the two of them in an intimate embrace, she knew the moment that it had been taken. Just seconds after Brian had held her and kissed her. Whoever had taken the photo had apparently observed their entire encounter.

Anger sent a rush of heat into her cheeks. Embarrassment followed. She felt exposed, violated. Shaken, Carrie pressed her hands together, straightened, and turned away from the newspaper.

"Great way to start the day, isn't it?" Brian said.

"I can't quite believe this."

Moving away from Brian, she paced the length of the kitchen, her bathrobe flapping open to reveal her shapely legs. Only vaguely aware of his intent gaze, she paused, her back to him as she stood in front of the French doors that led to the patio. She consciously summoned the effort required to calm herself and think rationally, but it took her a few minutes.

"I guess we need to speak with Detective Landis," Carrie remarked as she stared unseeing at the dense stand of Torrey pines that stood like sentries along the perimeter of her backyard.

"I've spoken to him."

"This morning?" she asked, turning to face him.

He approached her as he glanced at his watch. "Thirty minutes ago," he confirmed.

She recalled then Brian's effort to keep her from testifying during their conversation the previous day with Landis at police headquarters. His protective behavior had frustrated her. Although it still did to some degree, she was beginning to grasp his motives. "But the damage is already done if . . ." She couldn't complete the thought.

"I know."

Carrie started to tremble, more from outrage than from any real fear for her own well-being. She silently hoped that the two robbery suspects had already been taken into custody. She stared at Brian, not knowing what to say.

He suddenly reached for her.

She glimpsed understanding and several emotions she couldn't quite define as she blindly moved toward him. He encompassed her with his embrace, the scent of his skin, and the heat of his muscular body. She knew in her heart that he was merely offering her comfort and reassurance. He wasn't the kind of man who took advantage of a woman. That much she'd figured out.

Carrie felt the sweep of his broad-palmed

hands from her shoulders down the length of her spine, then the press of his fingertips at her waist when he shifted her closer. Despite the closeness of their bodies and the intimacy it implied, she trusted him the same way she'd trusted him during the robbery. She trusted him in spite of the very nearly reckless desire he inspired within her whenever he touched her.

She sank against him, too needful of the solidness and warmth he offered to do anything but ignore the voice in her head that urged her to step away from him and not tempt herself any further. She knew then the strength of the bond already forged between them. She knew as well how easy it would be to succumb to it. Carrie trembled within the circle of his strong arms, her mind shifting to the hours she'd spent in his embrace on the dance floor at the fund-raiser.

Foreplay.

There was no other word to describe the tension that had built between them. The net result had been feelings and sensations that had shimmered like an erotic rainbow through her body as they'd moved as one on the dance floor. Everything and everyone had faded to a peripheral blur. They might as well have been alone, she reflected, because no one one had intruded on them. Not once.

Drawing in a steadying breath, she lifted her head from Brian's shoulder and peered up at him. Her gaze lingered on his lips, acutely aware, as she had been the night before, that the time they'd spent dancing had been an education in sensory arousal and seduction.

She barely remembered driving herself home, but she knew she wouldn't ever forget Brian's searching kiss in the parking lot after he'd walked her to her car. She felt the appetite for intimacy that he'd awakened within her during their first minutes together rekindle deep inside her body. It seemed to expand with every passing moment, sucking her deeper and deeper into a whirling vortex of hope and need as she stared at his hard-featured face. She'd come perilously close to surrender the previous evening, but he'd refrained from pushing her, as though understanding her inner conflict and vulnerability.

They'd parted reluctantly, unvoiced regret, palpable desire, and several other unresolved issues lingering between them as they'd said good night.

The door chimes suddenly rang out again.

Carrie flinched, then moved out of Brian's arms.

"Get dressed."

His brusque order scraped like sandpaper across her sensitive emotions. She glared at him.

He closed the space she'd put between them and placed his hand on her shoulder. "Please get dressed. I asked Landis to meet me here."

Carrie nodded and slipped free of his hand,

but she paused and looked back at him from the arched kitchen doorway. "I won't be long."

"I'll work on the drill-instructor routine."

She managed a half smile. "See that you do."

Brian answered the door, the combined tension of the sexual desire thundering through his veins and his anger with the irresponsible behavior of the media evident in his tight expression as he greeted the detective. From the look of his rumpled clothes and furrowed brow, it seemed as if the detective hadn't left police headquarters since their meeting with him the previous morning. He offered Landis coffee before the two men walked out to the patio.

"Does she know yet about the newspaper article?" Landis asked.

"She knows," Brian confirmed. He made no effort to hide his anger.

"How's she handling it?"

"She's furious."

Landis nodded as he prowled up and down the length of the patio. "Not surprising."

"She won't back down, though."

"You tried to talk her out of testifying, didn't you?"

Brian strolled to the edge of the patio. "No, although I probably should have."

"It'll be a wasted effort," Landis predicted, still in motion.

Brian swore angrily. He knew the detective was right.

"What will be a wasted effort?" Carrie asked as she joined them on the patio.

Brian turned at the sound of her voice. He took in the shorts and T-shirt she wore, the quickly scrubbed face, and the absence of cosmetics. She didn't need the latter. She didn't need any adornment to enhance her natural appeal. She was the most seductive woman he'd ever met, and she didn't even realize it. God help him!

"Brian?"

Her voice pierced his thoughts. "Trying to persuade you not to testify," Brian answered.

Carrie's chin lifted a notch, stubbornness in the gesture and in her flashing eyes. "Don't waste your breath." She shifted her attention to Landis. "Good morning."

Landis stopped his agitated pacing. "I'm afraid it isn't a very good morning, Ms. Forbes."

She frowned, her fears confirmed. She asked the question poised on the tip of her tongue anyway. "You haven't taken the other two into custody yet, have you?"

"No, ma'am, we haven't."

Carrie glanced at Brian, then back at Landis. "Are you at all optimistic about finding them?" she asked.

Landis gave a moment of thought to her query before answering. "We're hopeful. They're leaving a trail a blind man could follow. It's almost as if they want us to find them."

"They want a confrontation."

"It would appear that way." Landis cleared his throat. "The risk to you could be very grave if they get to you before we nail them."

Brian grudgingly gave Landis points for honesty, but he remained silent. He sensed that anything he said to Carrie about rethinking her decision to testify would be met with resistance. He concluded then that his only real alternative was to find a way to keep her safe until the robbers were taken into custody.

"There is risk in every choice we make," Carrie observed with dignity.

Brian ended his silence. "What about the third witness?"

Landis exhaled heavily. "She took herself out of the game last night. Said her husband wouldn't permit her to testify even if all three are in custody throughout the trial."

"You expected that to happen," Carrie reminded him.

The detective nodded.

"What now?" Brian asked, although he suspected he already knew the answer.

Landis lowered himself onto a patio chair before he spoke. "Manpower in the department is stretched to the limit at present, so all I can offer is an increase in police visibility in your immediate neighborhoods."

"Drive-bys are useless, and you know it," Brian snapped.

Landis didn't argue the point. "I spoke to Field Agent Murphy after you and I talked this morning. He's trying to work something out with his people at the Bureau. I'm still waiting for a callback from him."

Carrie walked to the edge of the patio as Brian and Landis continued their conversation. Their voices faded to a low hum as she pressed her fingertips to her forehead, her memories from the past parading through her mind in spite of her desire to banish the events that had reshaped her life and altered her perceptions of herself during her final year of college. With her memories came the inevitable reminder of how paralyzing fear and helplessness could be.

This time, though, she felt no real sense of fear or helplessness. Just outrage. Pure, unadulterated outrage.

Carrie shuddered, unaware that Brian and Detective Landis had fallen silent and were watching her. Her memories played like a silent film in her mind as she stood there. She reminded herself that when she'd declined to participate in the prosecution of the man guilty of date-raping her two weeks before her twenty-first birthday, she'd allowed others to control her destiny, thereby robbing herself of vindication and closure. She'd learned too late the cost of that decision when she'd responded to her parents' urging that she not make a public spectacle of herself in open court by testifying.

She'd realized during her recovery that their concern had been for themselves, not her, although she hadn't wanted to believe the truth. But the truth had been in their eyes every time they'd looked at her, just as it had been in their voices when they'd spoken to her. They'd been ashamed, ashamed of their only child for putting herself—and them—in a position of notoriety and ridicule.

Her late mother had even gone so far as to observe that Carrie must have done something to cause the man to assault her. Those words, so casually spoken, had devastated her almost as much as the rape.

Conservative, monied, emotionally aloof, and far older than most parents of people her age, Louise and Grant Forbes had always gone to great lengths to guard their reputation within the community. The aftermath of the attack on their daughter had been no different. Her decision not to prosecute her rapist in a moment of weakness and self-doubt still haunted her, still made her view herself as a coward, but it also now fueled Carrie's refusal to be victimized by fear or the possibility of reprisal.

What her parents hadn't ever realized was that they'd destroyed her confidence in herself as a woman. They also hadn't lived long enough to witness her commitment to the Crisis Center and her work as a counselor. Nor would they ever know that she annually donated funds in their names from the estate they'd left to her. Poetic justice, she'd discovered, provided a modicum of satisfaction.

Carrie wondered periodically what her parents would have thought of the choices she'd made in the years since their deaths in a freak aircraft accident, but in her heart of hearts she knew the answer. They wouldn't approve, and that knowledge saddened her far more than their absence from her life.

She felt a hand slide across her shoulders, then recognized the weight and warmth of Brian's touch. Wiping the tears from her cheeks, she turned and looked up at him. She saw concern and compassion in his steady gaze, and she felt grateful that he didn't feel compelled to question her.

"Detective Landis has a cabin at Big Bear Lake," he told her. "He's offered us the use of it until the two robbery suspects are taken into custody."

"I'd rather stay in my own home. Can't something be arranged?" she asked.

"Not a good idea. We'd be sitting ducks. On a good day, we'll receive isolated moments of protection from police units patrolling the neighborhood, so it doesn't make any sense to stick to our normal routines while these guys are on the loose."

"What about the FBI? Surely they'd be willing

to provide guards. Agent Murphy made it clear that he wants these men prosecuted. He said as much to me when he took my statement."

"Landis is using your phone to call Murphy now. If they don't come up with a viable solution, you can be damn sure I will." Brian tugged her closer. "You all right?"

Carrie rested her head against his shoulder and closed her eyes. "Fine. No need to worry."

"I don't mind listening."

"I mind talking," she whispered.

"Later, then."

She said nothing. There would be no later.

Brian shifted her so that she stood before him. He lifted her chin with his fingertips. "We're in this together, so we need to work as a team."

Carrie searched his dark eyes. She marveled briefly over the dense, nearly black lashes that framed them, aware that every single one of her women friends would kill to possess such eyelashes, not just the man attached to them.

"Where are you?"

"Right here," she said, refocusing on his face. "And I agree with you. We need to act like a team, not like a king and his pawn."

Brian chuckled. "I thought you said I was a drill instructor."

"Take your pick. Both are control freaks."

Brian's expression lost its humor as he studied her. "Something's eating at you, Carrie. Something really serious. You don't have to deal with it alone."

She stiffened. "You're imagining things."

Brian opened his mouth to speak, but just at that moment Landis hurried through the French doors and out onto the patio.

"Good news," the detective announced. "Murphy's going to assign one of his people to the Big Bear cabin. He'll drive to the location in his RV and park at the edge of the lake, which is less than twenty yards from the cabin. Murphy picked him because he knows the area and is an avid fisherman. He'll fit in with the local flora and fauna."

Carrie picked that moment to admit the secret she'd kept from Brian since his arrival. "I received two breather calls between three and four this morning. They might be coincidence, or they might be your suspects. I thought you should know, Detective."

When she finished speaking, she refused to meet Brian's gaze. She didn't want to see his anger. She also didn't want to be told that she'd behaved foolishly. She already knew it.

Landis simply said, "Let's get you packed and out of here right away, Ms. Forbes. Better safe than sorry is my motto." He headed back into the house, calling out over his shoulder, "I need to make a few more calls."

Carrie stepped past Brian, intent on following Landis back into her house.

He caught her by the wrist and jerked her to a stop. "Why in hell didn't you tell me?"

"What would it have accomplished?"

"That isn't the point," he insisted.

"Then what is the point?"

"I want us to survive this mess. We can't do that if you keep secrets. It just makes us more vulnerable to two men who won't know a moment of regret if they kill the only witnesses willing to testify against them."

She sighed, not bothering to refute his comments. He was right, and she knew it. "I apologize. I won't do it again."

Brian drew her into his arms, his embrace fierce enough to bruise her ribs as he hugged her. "Why can't you get it into your head that I don't want anything to happen to you?"

Startled by his intensity, Carrie eased free of him. She absently massaged her wrist as she spoke. "I don't want anything to happen to either one of us."

SIX

Brian glanced at Carrie as he guided the car along the two-lane road carved out of the rugged San Bernadino Mountains. "Are you hungry? We can stop, if you'd like."

"Maybe later," she answered. "I don't have much of an appetite right now."

"You've been awfully quiet since we left San Diego," Brian observed as he downshifted into a hairpin curve.

Carrie shrugged. "Nothing to say, I guess." Her gaze roamed over the scenic vistas provided by the mountains.

Brian darted another look at her profile. He assumed that her thoughts were on the events that had taken place during and after the robbery. Because her life had been turned upside down, he told himself that she had every right to be distracted. He concluded that being forced to leave her home had simply enhanced her tension, even though he sensed that something totally unrelated to the robbery was bothering her.

Watching her earlier as she'd stood on the patio while he and Landis had talked, he'd promised himself that he would know the cause of her unease before the day ended. He renewed that promise now, albeit silently.

"It's been a rough week," Brian remarked, his tone of voice even.

She nodded. "True."

"Landis called the sheriff's substation at the lake while you were packing. They'll be alert to our presence during our stay at the cabin."

"That's good."

He reached out, took Carrie's hand, and gave it a reassuring squeeze. Despite the warm summer air streaming in from the open windows, her skin felt cold to the touch. He frowned. She withdrew her hand without a word, edging closer to the passenger door.

Brian realized then that she was pulling completely away from him. He wanted to understand why, but he managed to discard the idea of pressing for an explanation now. Despite his concern for her, he said little during the final hour of the trip. He knew they would have plenty of time to talk once they reached the cabin. He hoped that Carrie would be able to unwind then. He also hoped that she would trust him enough to confide in him. He didn't question why he wanted her trust, although he sensed he should.

He knew as well that a large part of his own inner tension was caused by the desire she provoked within him. He wanted her with every breath he took, his body pulsing with arousal each time he looked at her or touched her. If his response to her hadn't been so reckless, he might have laughed at himself. But there was nothing funny about his reaction to Carrie. She called into question the decision he'd made after his divorce to remain emotionally uninvolved, made him doubt that decision even though he knew in his gut that he was lousy relationship material.

Carrie's impact on him shocked him, because he couldn't recall a time in his life when he hadn't been able to exercise ruthless control over his feelings for any woman. Her very existence had blown that illusion of ironclad control to smithereens. She wasn't like his ex-wife or the other women in his past. Because she was an unknown quantity, he knew he needed to proceed with caution and restraint where she was concerned, in spite of his hunger to know her intimately.

His body refused, though, to comply with his common sense, the discomfort caused by the resurging desire he felt for her enough to make him grit his teeth as he drove. Taunted by her nearness and the now-familiar fragrance she wore, his desire throbbed heavily through his bloodstream in harmony with his pulse.

He felt relieved when he pulled up in front of the cabin, which had been easy to find thanks to the map Detective Landis had provided. Brian spotted the RV parked at the edge of the lake within seconds of exiting the car. He acknowledged the lone man seated in a lawn chair in front of the RV with a casual wave, which was returned.

He handed Carrie the key to the cabin's front door after helping her from the car. "Don't worry about the luggage and groceries," he suggested, referring in part to the supplies they'd purchased at a lakeside grocery store.

"That's all right." She reached for her suitcase when he opened the trunk, then made her way into the cabin.

Brian managed to contain his frustration with her aloof attitude. He walked the perimeter of the lakefront lot, then he introduced himself to the field agent Murphy had assinged to them. Brian judged the man competent once he realized that the agent had been thoroughly briefed by Murphy and was experienced enough to do his job unobtrusively.

He found Carrie unpacking groceries in the kitchen when he entered the rustic, two-bedroom cabin an hour later. They worked together, speaking infrequently as they prepared a tossed salad, steamed rice, and a simple chicken-and-sliced-vegetable stir-fry dish.

Carrie fell silent again during their meal, but she joined him to linger in front of the fireplace instead of retreating to her bedroom after they shared the cleanup chores. Brian breathed a quiet sigh of relief.

"Want a refill?" he asked before filling his empty wineglass.

Seated at the opposite end of the couch, she lifted her glass. "I still have some, but thanks." She gave him a fleeting smile before redirecting her gaze to the flames dancing above the logs in the native stone fireplace. "Having a fire was a good idea. I'd forgotten how quickly it cools down up here once the sun sets."

"You've been here before?"

"As a counselor with a church camp group when I was in college. It's still very beautiful, although more heavily populated."

"You seem more relaxed now," he remarked.

Carrie nodded and met his gaze once more. "I am. As you said in the car, it's been a rough week. I needed some time to get it all into perspective."

She searched his face then, acutely aware of the desire ribboning through her body like currents of supercharged energy. She trembled suddenly, the wine in the bottom of the glass she held sloshing back and forth.

"What's wrong?"

"Nothing," she whispered, embarrassed by her lack of control over herself and the direction of her thoughts.

As she studied Brian she felt nearly overwhelmed by her longing to touch and be touched by him. She wanted to feel his hands on her body, wanted to absorb his warmth and his strength into her pores, wanted to feel just once more the desire his powerful body had conveyed while they'd danced at the fund-raiser, and she wanted to sample again the heat and passion of his kiss. She wanted, as well, the freedom to explore him with her fingertips, although she couldn't remember ever wanting such a thing with any other man. The thought of tracing the lines and hollows of his muscular body sent a rush of dizzying desire into her veins and made her heart race.

As if sensing her state of wanting, Brian took her wineglass and placed it on the coffee table along with his.

She watched him from beneath half-lowered lashes, watched him with the wariness of a trapped animal. "What are you doing?" she asked, her heart galloping beneath her breasts.

She thought she might explode if he touched her, but that wild place inside her, that place she struggled to contain whenever they were together, wanted him so much, wanted his touch so intensely that she felt her entire body tremble with hopeful expectation.

"Tell me," she insisted, warning in her voice as she spoke.

He moved toward her. "Nothing you don't want me to do."

"Brian . . ."

"Come here," he urged, gently deflecting her hands when she tried to stave off his advance.

She sensed that stemming an advancing tide would be easier. "Please . . ."

He tugged her closer even as he shifted toward her. They came together in the center of the couch. Carrie stopped breathing for a long moment, hunger and uncertainty colliding deep inside her.

Peering down at her, he asked, "Please, what?"

"I can't do this. I can't give you—"

"I'm not asking you to give me anything. I just want to hold you."

He gathered her into his arms, so gently that she nearly burst into tears. She longed to trust him enough to surrender, but how could she? she wondered, even as she felt herself being consumed by the heat emanating from his large body. She exhaled, the air in her lungs rushing free of her body as she melted into him.

He meant it, she realized a little while later, although it stunned her. He kept his promise. He simply held her, his hands gentle as he caressed her back and shoulders, his breathing easy, and his heartbeat steady beneath her ear. His body reminded her of coiled steel, though, and that thought brought with it a rush of erotic visual images that shook her to her core.

Carrie relaxed in stages as he held her, shocking herself that she could. But she didn't believe in tempting fate indefinitely, and when she felt the muscles in his body tremble, heard his sharp intake of breath when she moved against his lower body without warning, she knew it was time to put some distance between them.

She knew he wanted her. She felt the telltale evidence of his arousal as he suddenly drew her up and into his lap. She couldn't ignore the condition of his body.

But he said nothing, did nothing. He looked at her, the strain he felt confined to the muscle ticking high in his cheek and in the darkening of his eyes.

Carrie caught her breath, her eyes locked on his, her fingertips digging into his shoulders as she held on to him. The air in her lungs burned for release once more, and she exhaled shakily.

"I don't intend to take anything from you that you're not prepared to give."

Her eyes widened. She wanted him, wanted him so desperately that she ached everywhere, but she knew that life wasn't that simple. Especially not for her.

Without warning, the disgust-filled voice of the man she'd almost married, the man whose insensitivity to her past had persuaded her that she wouldn't ever achieve the emotional or physical union with a man that she longed for, sounded in her head. She shivered, catapulted back to the past.

Although they'd been intimate several times

during their engagement, she realized once they'd gone their separate ways that she'd never completely trusted him. She hadn't run screaming from his bed, though. No. She hadn't run. She'd gone like a lamb to the slaughter instead, and she still felt like a fool for displaying such poor judgment.

She'd tried to be an accommodating lover. Unfortunately, she hadn't been as responsive as he'd expected, and he had reacted to her hesitation and lack of experience as if they were personal deficits, deficits he referred to whenever he couldn't provoke the kind of sexual response from her that he wanted. As a result of his careless cruelty, he'd devastated the fledgling confidence she'd managed to acquire in counseling in the years after the rape.

Carrie freed herself, scrambling from Brian's lap to stand between the couch and the coffee table.

He didn't attempt to stop her.

Carrie glanced at him. The regret and confusion she saw in his expression, not just the desire still darkening his eyes, made her pause and prompted her to attempt an explanation. "I . . . I'm tired. It's time for me to say good night."

Brian caught her hand. "Don't run from me. There's no need."

She stared at him. The warmth of his touch sank into her flesh, seducing her as effectively as if he'd stroked her entire body with his fingertips.

"Why are you afraid of me?" he asked.

"I'm not," she insisted.

He refused to release her. "Then what?"

"Myself," Carrie whispered in a moment of stark honesty. "I'm afraid of myself."

Brian frowned. "Why?"

I want more than I'll ever have, she nearly shouted, but she managed to quell her response. She squared her shoulders. "I meant what I said earlier. I can't give you what you want."

"I haven't asked you for anything," he quietly reminded her.

"You will."

He got to his feet.

"I'm going to bed now, Brian. Alone."

"I know that." He settled his hands on her shoulders.

"Then let me go." She felt the sweep of his gaze as he searched her features.

"I can't, Carrie. I just can't," he finally confessed as he drew her forward, cupped her face between his hands, and brought his mouth down to hers.

She started to protest by saying his name, but the first syllable didn't make it past her lips before he claimed them, gently at first, then with greater possessiveness.

She gasped, hunger bursting to life within her like a suddenly flaring torch. Shock shimmied through her, then rocked her to the depths of her soul and battered her weary heart.

She felt his hands skim down her back, settle briefly at her waist, and the move over her hips, measuring, shaping, then testing the fit of their bodies as he gathered her closer and reacquainted her with the strength of his hard loins. A moan escaped her, but the sound wasn't even remotely connected to panic.

So aroused that she nearly whimpered when he anchored her hips to his, she gripped his shirt-front. Brian made a reassuring sound and smoothed her hands upward before deepening their kiss. She tangled her fingers at his nape and surged even closer, craving the contact as instincts she didn't even know she possessed guided her. Her breasts flattened against the hard wall of his chest, her nipples, already taut buds of sensation, tightening into points of near pain that ached for his touch.

Carrie willingly parted her lips and angled her head, welcoming the thrust of his tongue as it darted repeatedly into her mouth. She sank into his passion, the mindlessness of her need forcing her beyond the emotional and sexual boundaries she'd always imposed on herself.

She shuddered, twisting into him so that the hard ridge of his maleness throbbed against her lower abdomen. Instead of being unnerved by the obvious arousal of his body, she couldn't seem to get enough of him, couldn't seem to get close enough, couldn't find a way to satisfy the soul-deep yearning that had hidden like a ready-to-pounce tiger within her for so many years.

Chemistry.

She finally understood the meaning of the word as Brian ate at her lips and ravaged her mouth. His hands roamed over her, inciting flash fires of response.

She stopped fighting the inevitability of her own desire, stopped resisting the impulse to surrender, stopped trying to thwart her feminine instincts. The futility of her attempt to sit on the sidelines of life suddenly cascaded over her, and she realized that she needed to try, needed to trust, not just this man, but herself.

She discovered courage in that moment of recognition. Carrie Forbes accepted the fact that she couldn't sustain her single-person campaign for survival any longer. She needed to live. She needed to feel. And she desperately needed to love. She needed, she realized, the emotional nourishment of caring and being cared for. And in the final analysis, she needed Brian York for an extremely simple reason—she was falling in love with him.

Brian wrenched his mouth free moments later, startling her with his abruptness. He gripped her shoulders as she stared up at him, his breathing ragged, his face all hard angles and tense lines when he finally met her gaze.

"I cannot believe what you do to me," he managed to mutter through gritted teeth.

"I want you," she said before she could stop herself.

"I've never wanted a woman more." He embraced her, shuddering violently against her.

She felt the leashed power of his body, and knew again that he was a man of honor. He wouldn't ever force her. *Be honest with him*, a voice in her head urged, and so she tried. "I haven't wanted anyone for a very long time."

"That's a two-way street."

"Is it?"

He nodded.

"Why?" she asked.

His gaze grew distant, as though he'd glimpsed disillusionment in its purest form in the privacy of his mind. "It just is."

Carrie suddenly realized that she wasn't the only one in the cabin burdened by baggage from the past. Brian obviously had some of his own.

"It's hard to trust, isn't it?" he observed.

"Very hard," she agreed.

"I want you, but I don't want to push you into something you're not sure you want."

"I'm not sure, in spite of how my body feels right now."

"I understand."

She studied him for a moment. "I really think you do."

"Our situation is pretty unconventional."

"It's totally crazy, and we shouldn't complicate it any more than it already is."

"I want you."

"I still want you," she admitted, surprised that she could articulate her desire for him with such honesty. "But I'm afraid I'd only disappoint you, Brian, and that's the last thing I want to do. I've learned my limits and tolerances over the years. I'm not like most women."

"Talk to me, Carrie. Tell me what's wrong."

His sensual voice. She would hear the sound of it in her dreams for the rest of her life, she realized. Half in love with him already and feeling half out of her mind thanks to the desire coursing through her bloodstream, she struggled for the right words to explain her behavior. In the end, though, she failed to find them.

"Nothing's wrong."

"You're pulling away from me."

Her eyes fell closed as she bowed her head and pressed her fingertips to her forehead. She felt something precious inside of herself start to shatter, and she prayed that it wasn't her newly discovered courage. Exhaustion washed over her, the kind of emotional and physical fatigue that made her wonder if she shouldn't be living in a bubble. Safe. Separate. Protected from the world.

"Please don't pull away."

She lifted her face from her hands and looked at him. "I need to right now. I feel like I'm coming apart at the seams."

"Why?" he asked, his hands sliding around her narrow waist.

He gripped her so tightly that she knew she'd find fingerprint bruises there by morning. "I'd only disappoint you."

"Disappoint me?"

She read the disbelief in his gaze. "Trust me, I would. That's the long and short of it, I'm afraid. I'd disappoint you, so let's back up ten paces and return to being witnesses to a bank robbery."

"There's a hell of a lot more going on here besides a damn bank robbery," he said angrily, "and we both know it."

"Please let go of me," she said, sadness resonating in her voice.

He honored her plea, but Carrie didn't miss his reluctance.

She turned away from him and made her way out of the cabin's living room. By the time she reached her bedroom, slipped inside, and closed the door, her knees were shaking. She sank down onto the edge of the bed and wept, the desire and the emotional despair she felt contained in every beat of her heart and in every ragged breath she took.

SEVEN

"Let's take a walk," Brian suggested the next morning after he spent almost a solid hour prowling the interior of the cabin.

"Good idea." Carrie set aside her magazine and surged to her feet. "The walls are starting to close in on me."

He waited while she found her shoes and put them on. After locking the front door, he tucked the key into his jacket pocket and took her hand.

They spotted the FBI agent as they made their way to the edge of the lake, but they didn't join him. Seemingly intent on his fishing, the agent nodded when he saw them and returned his attention to the endeavor.

Thick clouds of surface fog clung to the lake and the surrounding landscape, obscuring both the pines that extended for miles in every direction and the mountain peaks that had been visible at the time of their arrival the previous afternoon. A light mist dampened the clean air. Chattering blue jays periodically disturbed the quiet of the morning, but no other sounds penetrated the dense foliage.

"Did you get any sleep last night?" Brian asked several minutes into their walk.

Carrie shot him a rueful smile. "A little. How about you?"

"About the same."

"I should probably apologize for what happened. I let you think . . ." Carrie paused. "I'm not usually so . . . reckless."

"You weren't reckless at all," Brian insisted.

"Thank you for understanding and not pushing me."

"Believe me, I was tempted."

"But you didn't, Brian, and that meant a lot to me."

He glanced at her. "My wanting you isn't going to end anytime soon." If ever, he amended silently.

She exhaled, the sound as soft as a whisper. "We don't always get what we want, do we?"

"Reality. It sucks some of the time."

His blunt remark, so unexpected, made her laugh out loud, but the sound died in her throat as quickly as it had begun when she heard something pop.

Eyes wide with disbelief, Carrie stumbled to a stop and looked around.

They heard two more pops.

She cringed.

"What the . . ." Brian began, not believing his ears. He grabbed Carrie, his hand settling heavily on her shoulder.

More pops.

She groaned like an abused animal. "No! No! No!" she cried, wrenching free of him.

Brian didn't stop to think. He reacted instinctively to Carrie's distress and the sound of discharging weapons. He lifted her into his arms and raced across the narrow glade they'd entered just moments before. Spotting a sheltered area beneath the nearest stand of pines ahead of them, he made a beeline for it.

Carrie fought him every step of the way, twisting in his arms and beating at his shoulders with her fists.

Unprepared for her resistance, Brian managed to subdue her with his superior strength without hurting her. Once he reached the trees, he lowered her to stand in front of him and steadied her while she regained her footing.

Shoving his hands aside, she escaped him and darted out of range, her expression panicked.

Brian went after her.

Additional shots rang out, much closer this time. Where in the hell was Agent Hill? he wondered.

Carrie halted suddenly. Brian clamped one hand on her shoulder and looped his other arm around her waist. As he yanked her back against his chest she screamed.

Desperate to silence her so that she wouldn't draw attention to their location, Brian tackled her, forcing her to the ground as he tried to contain her flailing limbs.

She landed hard, the air in her lungs rushing out of her body. Although struggling to breathe, she didn't stop fighting him. She bucked beneath him, trying to dislodge the weight of his large body as he flattened her against the damp earth.

"Dammit, Carrie!"

Her frenzied movements persisted. Brian felt as if he'd been thrown into a cage with a wildcat. He wanted to understand the reason for her behavior, but he remained focused on keeping her alive and safe if the bank-robbery suspects had somehow managed to find their hideaway.

Eyes closed, head thrown back, Carrie pounded at his shoulders with her fists. Strangled whimpers escaped her. As Brian glanced around he tried to soothe her with reassuring words, but she seemed lost in a nightmare he didn't comprehend.

His next thought came out of nowhere. He felt the chill of it right down to his soul. Carrie Forbes had acted like the victim of a violent assault. Nothing else made sense, he realized, recalling a woman friend who'd survived a mugging while traveling abroad, and remembering as well how many years it had taken her to find her way back to a normal life.

Brian knew in his gut that nothing else could explain Carrie's response to his attempts to get her out of harm's way—at the bank and here at the lake. He died a little inside, and several moments elapsed before he registered the sudden, nearly deafening stillness that had settled over the forest.

He shook himself free of his thoughts and searched the surrounding terrain as the quiet completely penetrated his consciousness. Then he looked at Carrie, and what he saw broke his heart.

Her skin was pale, and tears streaked her cheeks. The memory of some past terror still clouded the normally brilliant color of her eyes.

She trembled beneath him, her gaze riveted on his face as she tried to catch her breath. "I'm sorry," she gasped out as she wept. "Oh, God, I'm so sorry."

"It's all right, Carrie," he assured her as he pressed a kiss to her forehead. "I won't let anything happen to you . . . not ever."

She gave him a bewildered look that made him think of a child emerging from a bad dream. "I thought . . . I don't know what I thought."

Brian exhaled, grateful that she'd come back to herself. Later, he promised himself, they would talk. Later he would know the truth, but for now he intended to protect her with his life.

They both stiffened when they heard someone

or something crashing through the underbrush not far from their hiding place.

Brian gave her a warning glance.

Carrie closed her eyes and gripped his shoulders.

"York! This is Hill speaking," shouted the man assigned to guard them. "It's all clear. You can come out now."

Brian recognized Hill's distinctive Boston accent. Some of his worry departed, but he remained wary. Settling more heavily against Carrie, he wrapped his arms around her, gathered her against his chest, and buried his face in the scented curve between her neck and shoulder.

She struggled, but halfheartedly. "Brian."

"We need to stay put for a few more minutes."

"All right, but you're crushing me."

He eased the pressure of his weight by bracing his upper body on his elbows, but his loins remained fitted to the welcoming curves and hollows of her parted thighs. He soon felt the escalating heat generated by their close contact as it winnowed into his bloodstream, but he swiftly quelled his reaction to Carrie by sheer force of will. The last thing he wanted to do was make her feel helpless by inflicting his aroused anatomy on her at a time like this.

"York!" Hill shouted yet again. "Answer me. I need to know if you're all right."

Brian continued to ignore the man. As he studied Carrie he noticed that some of the natural color had returned to her cheeks and that her tears had ceased. "Better?" he asked.

"Better, thank you."

"Your manners are showing," he teased.

Carrie shrugged. "So sue me."

"Smartmouth," he accused, relief flowing into him that she sounded like herself again.

"Pure reflex," she informed him. "Just like your drill-instructor routine."

Brian grinned at her.

"York? Where the hell are you?"

"Aren't you going to answer him?" she asked.

His grin disappeared. "In a minute. I'm more concerned about you. Are you really all right?"

Carrie nodded. "I think so."

"What happened? A flashback of some kind?"

She stared at him before her gaze drifted to a spot above his head. Her chin trembled as she struggled for control.

Brian saw the answer to his question in her haunted hazel eyes when she finally refocused on his face. He knew with absolute certainty at that moment that she'd been the victim of an assault. As he grappled with the realization he prayed that she hadn't been raped. He feared that she had been, though. Her reaction whenever she was physically overpowered added fuel to his certainty, as did her work as a crisis counselor. Who better to help the damaged, he asked himself, than someone who'd been damaged herself?

"York? Ms. Forbes? You aren't in any danger.

A couple of kids decided to try out their rifles in a restricted area. I've disarmed them, and everything's under control now. I've already radioed the sheriff's substation."

Brian spotted and recognized Hill's red leather cowboy boots as he peered through the underbrush. Easing free of Carrie, he helped her to her feet. Twigs and leaves clung to her thick auburn hair and casual clothes. He brushed her off with the impersonal touch of a doctor, then hugged her when she finished doing the same for him.

"York! Dammit, man, you can show yourself now. It's safe."

"We're over here," Brian announced. Claiming Carrie's hand, he led her out of the shelter provided by the centuries-old pine trees.

Hill greeted them with a shamefaced expression. "I'm really sorry about what just happened. Those kids took me completely by surprise." He peered at Carrie. "Ma'am, are you okay?"

Carrie nodded. "Of course."

Brian thought she still looked pale and shaken, but he kept his opinion to himself.

Still inspecting Carrie, Hill said, "Please let me escort you back to the cabin. It's the least I can do after what's happened."

Brian slipped his arm around Carrie's waist and drew her into his strength and heat. "No need, Hill. I'll take care of Ms. Forbes. I assume you'll deal with the boys."

Hill nodded. "If it's any consolation, they're

handcuffed to the bumper of the RV. I'll be turning them over to the sheriff's office as soon as the deputies arrive. Charges will be filed against them."

Carrie eased free of Brian. "I need the key, please."

He handed it to her. After watching her walk away, he peered at Hill, his expression glacial. "Nothing more can happen to her. She's already relived her own personal version of hell. She shouldn't have to do it again."

Hill swore, his understanding of Brian's comments obvious.

Neither man said anything more as they made their way along the rambling path that led to the cabin. Hill headed for his RV and the two sullen-looking teenagers handcuffed to the vehicle. Brian went in search of Carrie. He wondered as he entered the cabin what it would take to get her to open up and confide in him.

Brian found her in the kitchen, staring out the window above the sink as she drank a glass of water. As he silently debated the best way to initiate the conversation he felt compelled to have with her, he noticed that she'd brushed the rest of the leaves and twigs from her hair and clothing.

Carrie exhaled softly before turning to face him. "I owe you an explanation."

"You don't *owe* me anything, but I care enough about you to want to understand your reactions to things. And to me," he added, the admission making him feel unexpectedly vulnerable.

Brian realized in a moment of total honesty with himself that he cared more about her than he'd ever cared about another human being. Although thrown off balance by the depth of his feelings for her, he set aside his own emotional uneasiness and concentrated on Carrie.

"I do think we need to talk," he said as he approached her. "If you're willing, that is."

The haunted look back in her eyes, she squared her shoulders and lifted her chin. Brian watched her gather up her strength.

As he studied her he saw once again her innate courage. He'd glimpsed it before, particularly at the bank. He sensed the difficult battle she'd waged to reach deep inside of herself in order to survive a tragedy that would have destroyed a weaker person.

"Why don't we sit down?" Carrie suggested as she stepped past him and walked out of the kitchen. "This is going to take a while."

Brian followed her to the couch in front of the fireplace. Unlike the night before, there was no fire. But like the night before, he suspected that whatever they shared now would determine the next step in their relationship. He made no move to touch her once they made themselves comfortable on the couch. He didn't want to crowd her.

When Carrie extended her hand, he took it and brought it to his lips. He pressed a kiss to her knuckles before clasping her hand between both of his.

"There's no easy way to say this, so I'm just going to say it straight out. I was date-raped during my senior year of college," she announced.

Brian clenched his jaw, the rage and anguish that rose up inside of him almost too powerful to contain. For Carrie's sake, though, he managed to control himself. He tightened his grip on her, consciously sharing his strength in the only way he knew how.

"I'd known him for almost two years. We'd dated casually, but we were never lovers. He'd been having an on-again, off-again affair with a mutual friend. Anyway, he invited me to an outdoor concert in the park one evening. It was just before finals were about to start. The weather was perfect, the night sky was filled with twinkling stars, and the air was rich with the scent of hibiscus blossoms." She shook her head. "It's amazing how many of the details I still remember."

Carrie fell silent for several moments, as though to marshal her courage for what she was about to reveal.

Needing to offer comfort, Brian asked, "Will you let me hold you while we talk?"

She smiled, but the expression on her face was tinged with sadness. "I'd like that. In spite of the warm weather, I'm feeling chilled."

He carefully slipped his arm around her shoulders, relief flooding him when he felt her relax against his body.

Carrie looked up. "I won't break, Brian."

He nodded and gave her a fierce hug. "I'm glad you aren't afraid of me."

"You've never frightened me. Please believe that. What unnerved me . . . what still unnerves me . . . is how much I want you."

Her candor stunned him. He couldn't help wondering how she managed it, and he found himself envying the unique ability. "Do you still want me?" he asked before he realized how selfish he sounded.

"Very much, and I'm struggling with how to handle it." Looking away, she picked up where she'd left off. "I packed a picnic supper that night, and he brought a bottle of wine. Several people we knew were at the concert, so we all sat together in groups on the blankets we'd spread out on a grassy knoll overlooking the stage. The evening started out so nicely. The bands were incredible. Everyone was happy. I remember the sound of laughter. So much laughter." She pressed her fingertips to her forehead, as if trying to sort out and reconcile the mix of good and bad memories.

"Anyway, I didn't like the wine. It was too sweet, so I switched to iced tea. Rick wound up drinking most of the bottle. As the evening unfolded he seemed to grow moodier and moodier, but I didn't pay much attention because I was enjoying the music too much. I do remember thinking that he was probably still depressed about Mandy, the girl he'd broken up with, so I didn't say anything about his drinking. I did decide that I'd be the one to drive us home, even though his car had a stick shift and I hated them."

Carrie rested her head against Brian's shoulder as she spoke. "I'd left my car at his apartment, so I drove us there when the concert ended around midnight. A lot of the things he said didn't make any sense, but I chalked it up to the ramblings of a drunk. I recall feeling glad that we weren't anything more than friends, because I always felt uncomfortable around him whenever he drank too much. I even decided that I wouldn't see him again socially. He wasn't my type to start with, and we really didn't have much in common other than the fact that we'd been classmates for several semesters.

"I should never have gone into his apartment with him. I felt uneasy the minute I walked into the place, but he insisted that he had a book I'd need while I prepared for finals. He was talking so loud that I was afraid he'd wake the neighbors, so I let him persuade me to go inside while he looked for the book."

"Can I get you anything?" Brian asked when she paused. "Another glass of water, maybe?"

"Thank you, no." Carrie cleared her throat, but her voice sounded fragile as she moved forward with her memories. "I was a virgin, and I'd lived a very sheltered life up until that night. I couldn't have been more unprepared or more shocked when he grabbed me and shoved me against the hallway wall. I was frightened and I struggled, but he wouldn't let me go. I screamed. He hit me and then started shaking me and yelling at me. I went limp. Some part of my mind told me it was the only way to get him to stop. I was wrong. It just made him angrier, and he started hitting me again. I'd never been the object of anyone's violence, and the helpless feeling that came over me was staggering."

Tears slipped from her eyes as she lifted her face to look at Brian. "He knocked me unconscious. When I woke up . . . when I . . ." She sighed raggedly. "He'd finished with me by then."

Brian gathered her into his arms, positioning her in his lap. "You don't have to say anything more."

She buried her face against his neck until her tears waned. "I need you to understand."

"I do," he managed, his emotions in an uproar. "My God, I do."

". . . I hurt everywhere when I woke up. I couldn't believe the pain." She eased back to look at him, drew in a shattered breath, then released it. "He'd passed out on the floor of the hallway, so I pulled my clothes together and crawled to the front door. I felt as if I was moving in slow motion as I made my way to my car, and I could barely see out of my right eye. It took me a while to realize that it was swollen shut. I still don't remember driving myself to the hospital, but I managed to get there. Everything after that was a blur. It wasn't until I woke up the next morning and remembered what had happened that I started to unravel emotionally. I started screaming. The sound kept bouncing off the walls and slamming into me until a nurse gave me a sedative."

"Where is he?" Brian demanded, his tone of voice making it clear that retribution was in his mind.

She waved her hand dismissively. "I have no idea, and I don't want to know. He's not important any longer."

He peered at her and saw that she meant it, although his need for revenge made it hard to accept.

Carrie met his gaze. "I cooperated with the police once I became coherent enough to make a statement, then I worked with the district attorney's office, in spite of how excruciating it was to keep reliving what had happened. He was taken into custody, charges were filed. You know the procedure. Anyway, shortly before the trial was about to start, my parents persuaded me not to testify. They didn't want their reputations tarnished by the humiliation of seeing their daughter as the star witness in a very public rape trial, even though at the time they insisted that I wasn't strong enough to handle the proceedings. They hammered on me long enough to convince me that I'd be doing myself more harm than good. I was in counseling then, and I desperately needed their support, but I knew I wouldn't get it if I testified against him. So I caved in to their pressure, and I lived to regret it. For a long time afterward I hated them for not backing me up, but the hate is gone now. It's been replaced by pity. They were weak, self-indulgent people. They didn't have a clue about how badly they undermined my self-confidence or that my recovery took twice as long as it had to thanks to their selfishness."

The pieces of the puzzle fit together perfectly. He remained silent, though. Carrie's commitment to the Crisis Center, her determination to testify against the robbery/homicide suspects, her resistance to his advances, and her lack of sexual sophistication, which had been clear to him since the first time he'd touched her, now made perfect sense.

"Once I started to function like a person instead of like a victim, I returned to college. I stayed in counseling for several years, though, and it helped me come to terms with a lot of my feelings, especially the sense of powerlessness that I felt during and after the rape. I decided to become a counselor as a means of dealing with what had happened to me, because I was determined to help victims of sexual assault reclaim their lives and achieve some kind of closure. Surviving an act of violence like rape is one of the roughest experiences a person can endure, and it takes a support network provided by a place like the Crisis Center, which is why it's been the focus of my life for ten years now."

"Have you been with a man since the rape?" Brian asked quietly. He feared her response, but he needed the answer to his question.

She nodded. "Of course. I was serious when I said I'd come to terms with my feelings. Resolution was crucial to my survival, and I knew it. I worked harder than anyone will ever know to move beyond the emotional paralysis caused by the rape. I told you I'd been engaged. Bill and I were lovers for several months before our engagement was announced by our families. He was the son of one of my father's business associates, and our parents were longtime friends. But I . . . disappointed him in bed, and he became more and more harsh in his judgment of me. Having my sexual performance critiqued was humiliating. I ended the engagement. Looking back, I realize that he lacked the sensitivity and patience I want from a man. He would have been a terrible parent if we'd had children."

He voiced the obvious questions. "Are you willing to try again, Carrie, or are you afraid to make love?"

She shook her head. "I'm not afraid of making love, although I have to admit that I was for the first few years after the assault. Now I want a normal relationship and everything that goes with it, more than anything, but . . ."

"But what?" he asked, his voice filled with compassion as he clasped her hands.

"I guess I've never found the right man."

"Then what still frightens you?"

She studied him for several long moments before answering. "Two things. Being overpowered physically without any warning is the first thing, which I doubt surprises you. It troubles me that I haven't been able to master the panic I feel. I think I need a little more work in that area." She paused then and looked down at their joined hands.

"It explains your reaction to me at the bank and a little while ago. What else?" he asked, his grip on her tightening.

She met his gaze with tear-filled eyes. "I care about you. I care so very much, but my self-confidence about physical intimacy is pretty shaky. It would kill me if I disappointed you, Brian. It would just kill me to fail again, especially with you."

He felt humbled by her honesty. He didn't completely understand how someone who'd endured a violent sexual assault had the capacity to worry about the needs or desires of a potential lover. Few women in his experience possessed that kind of emotional generosity, but then Carrie Forbes wasn't like most women. He'd figured that out during the robbery.

That she cared for him gave him hope, but it also unsettled him. Speaking quietly, he told her,

"You're the most sensual woman I've ever held in my arms, and I seriously doubt that you'd ever disappoint me."

Carrie stared at him. "You sound so sure. How can you be so sure?"

"I've never been more sure of anything in my life, for one very simple reason. You trust me."

"Of course I trust you. I wouldn't be here if I didn't, but what does that have to do with the price of rice?" she demanded.

He smiled at her sudden outburst.

"This isn't even remotely funny, Brian. I don't want to be some kind of cripple for the rest of my life."

"You're remarkable, not crippled."

"Remarkable?" She shook her head. "Hardly."

Brian saw the disbelief etched into her expressive features, heard it resonate in the two words she'd just spoken, but he said nothing more. Instead, he gathered her against his chest and held her, savoring the woman, her strength, and the fact that she'd trusted him enough to share the truth of her past.

Carrie eventually relaxed and looped her arms around his shoulders.

Trust, Brian reflected, turning the word over in his mind. Carrie trusted him. Nothing had ever meant more to him, and he knew in his heart that it was a beginning.

He grappled, though, with the doubt that had plagued him since his divorce. Could he risk trusting his feelings for her? Could he risk exposing her to his well-documented failings as a partner in a committed relationship? Was he even capable of the kind of emotional accessibility she deserved? Harming or disappointing Carrie was the last thing he wanted to do.

EIGHT

Carrie glanced up from her book as Brian walked into the cabin's living room carrying an armload of firewood. The tension between them had steadily increased during the two days they had been there, but it was the tension of awareness between a man and a woman who desired each other—nothing more.

As she watched Brian arrange the lengths of wood on the grate in the fireplace, she thought again about his reaction to their conversation about her past. Because he'd responded with compassion and reassurance, instead of being put off by the truth, she felt accepted and unjudged.

Her original conclusions about Brian had been accurate. He was a man of character and integrity.

As she sat there she recalled that few of her friendships from the past had endured in the aftermath of the assault. Some people simply hadn't known how to treat her or talk to her. Nothing she'd tried to do had alleviated their discomfort. In the end, she'd relinquished those strained relationships and moved forward into the future. The Crisis Center served to ease the transition.

Other people, she discovered, were destined to link her to the experience and to view her as a victim. She'd seen it in their eyes, heard it when they'd asked intrusive, thoughtless questions. She loathed being cast in the role of victim, then and now. Still others had assumed she'd provoked the assault. They'd said as much. Their responses had forced her to rethink her expectations of people and had prompted her to fiercely guard her personal life during the intervening years.

Brian whistled tunelessly and knelt at the edge of the hearth. She smiled, watching as he added kindling and wadded-up newspaper to the firewood, then put a flame to the arrangement. After tucking the book of matches into his pocket, he straightened and turned away from the fireplace. He paused when he noticed her intent stare.

Carrie met his gaze, captivated not for the first time by the unmistakable changes that took place in his expressive face whenever he looked at her. She noticed that his eyes always darkened until they seemed almost black, and his angular features became even more defined, the structure of his face reminding her of a rough granite carving.

He never tried to conceal his desire. It was always there, on the surface, in his touch, and in his tone of voice when he spoke to her. The honesty of his response still startled her, but it empowered her as well. She felt stimulated and tantalized at the prospect of experiencing his passion. Fear had never been an issue for her with Brian. She doubted it ever would be. She sensed within herself a growing confidence that she would be able to embrace him, physically and emotionally, without any inhibitions if they became lovers. Her pulse leaped as images of the two of them making love formed in her mind.

Carrie gripped her book, only then realizing that she still held it in her hands. She exhaled shakily and put it aside. Reading, as well as any other activity meant to help the time pass more quickly until they heard from Detective Landis, was next to impossible when Brian was nearby.

Brian York was the kind of man she'd waited for her entire life. He was the lover she'd fantasized about during the years she'd spent alone, the friend and ally she'd longed for, and the confidant she'd needed.

She trembled as his gaze moved over her body and left a trail of tingling sensation. She felt as though she'd been caressed by invisible fingers. The hunger she experienced in the breathless moments that followed sent heat rushing through her veins and to the surface of her skin.

She felt sensitized, not just immobilized, by the extent of her desire for Brian. Transfixed by his stare, she knew she'd never wanted a man more than she wanted him, although she sensed his reluctance to exert any sexual-performance pressure. While she appreciated his patience, the growing need she felt to experience intimacy with him threatened to swamp her.

Other than when they slept in their separate bedrooms, they lived in each other's pockets in the small cabin. She constantly battled the impulse to reach out and touch him. She felt as tightly strung as a drawn bow most of the time, and the feeling frayed her nerves.

"You're staring," Brian remarked. His voice sounded brittle. It was the voice she associated with the self-control he felt compelled to exercise over himself when he wanted her.

Unable to stop herself, she let her gaze dip. His body revealed just how much he wanted her. As much, she concluded as she grappled with the river of flame steaming through her veins, as she wanted him.

"You're staring, Carrie," he said once more, his tone sharper this time.

She blinked. "You're right, I am."

Crossing the room, he took a seat at the opposite end of the couch. "Why?"

"I like the view."

He chuckled at her flippant remark, but there was a rueful quality to the sound of his humor.

Carrie couldn't quite believe the words that had just fallen out of her mouth.

"Relax, I feel the same way."

"I understand," she whispered.

"I'm hungry for you, so damned hungry that I wonder if my appetite will ever be satisfied."

She lapsed into silence. She'd never had this kind of a conversation with a man before, and she didn't know the rules—if there were any rules, she amended.

"I can't seem to help myself," he continued. "It's been a lot of years since I wanted a woman as much as I want you."

She glanced at him, then shifted her attention back to the darting flames around the stack of logs in the fireplace. "I've never wanted anyone so much, either."

"You're wondering why I'm holding back, aren't you?"

"I'm a little curious," she admitted.

"You're a lot curious, and we both know it."

"You're right," she conceded.

"I don't intend to rush you."

She nodded as she searched for the courage necessary to voice her next thought. "Perhaps you're worrying too much, and you shouldn't be so careful."

Brian muttered a curse. "I'm doing what's best for both of us. Besides, we'll both know when the time is right."

Without considering the wisdom of her actions, Carrie moved across the width of the couch to sit beside him. She felt a little like a homing pigeon, but she refused to resist the impulse or the need to be closer to him any longer.

Brian slid his arm around her shoulders and tugged her into his heat. She shivered slightly, even though his body reminded her of a furnace set on high. When she glanced up at him, she nearly drowned in the depths of his eyes.

No man had ever looked at her with such unabashed desire, and no man had ever evoked an answering desire within her heart or body. She felt consumed by it at moments like these. Irrevocably consumed. She sucked in a ragged breath.

His gaze narrowed. "What are you thinking about right now?"

"That we don't need that fire tonight. I'm already quite hot."

Brian shook his head. "You've got a real mouth on you, Ms. Forbes."

Turning in the circle of his arms, she leaned into him, hungry for the feel of him. She relaxed, delighting a moment later when she heard the raw sound that escaped him as her breasts plumped against his chest.

He gripped her upper arms, moving her back and forth so that her breasts rubbed against the hard wall of his chest. His eyes fell closed, and he inhaled a sharp-sounding breath.

Carrie almost cried out her frustration, but she bit back the sound even though her breasts ached for his hands. She felt her nipples tighten into tiny daggers of sensation. She wondered then how he would react if she confessed her curiosity about what it would feel like to have his mouth suckling the taut tips.

She felt a quickening deep inside her body, the sensation familiar to her only because she experienced it whenever Brian touched her. No one had ever evoked such tumultuous feelings within her. She rested her forehead against his chin. Shaken, she didn't speak.

He held her for several minutes, the raggedness of his breathing eventually evening out. "I still can't quite believe how I feel when I hold you."

She lifted her face and met his gaze. "I love the way I feel when you touch me."

A muscle ticked high in his jaw. "Careful," he warned.

Bemused by his tone, she asked the obvious question. "Why?"

"I'm already on fire for you."

She grinned, delighted by his response. It fueled her fragile confidence even more. "There's an extinguisher in the kitchen. I could get it for you, if you'd like."

"Nice," he said with a growl before drawing her forward and nuzzling her neck with his lips. "Real nice. I'm going to have to do something about your mouth."

"You could always kiss me. That would shut me up."

"Don't tempt me," he murmured, his hot

breath washing across the sensitive skin of her neck.

Carrie moaned, her head tipping sideways and her fingers tangling at his nape as he nibbled at her skin and sent erotic messages to her brain and other very specific regions of her body. "Are you paying me back for some imagined slight?" she asked breathlessly.

He lifted his head, his gaze scorching her as he searched her features. "I'm not into revenge, just payback."

With that comment, he claimed her mouth, his tongue thrusting past her lips and even white teeth to penetrate the heated depths beyond. She gasped, then angled her head even more to welcome his exploration.

She felt his hold on her tighten, felt the tremors that rippled through his large body, felt the corresponding quakes deep inside herself. She gripped his broad shoulders, her fingertips kneading rhythmically. She savored the taste of him as it saturated her senses and sent her spinning into a world of kaleidoscopic colors and lights.

Moaning into his mouth, Carrie surrendered to both the possessive sweep of his hands as they moved over her and to the erotic lessons he gave her with his tongue and lips. She responded eagerly to the intimate foray he conducted, answering his inciteful passion with unrestrained response.

Their tongues tangled, the heated duel that

ensued arousing her to a feverish state. She slid her hands across his shoulders and then down his chest, her fingertips absorbing the fierce pounding of his heart even before she tugged his T-shirt free of the waistband of his jeans. Free to conduct a tactile exploration of her own, she skimmed her fingertips up his flat belly, then tunneled her fingers into the dense pelt of hair that covered his broad chest. She felt every shudder her touch provoked.

She felt more feminine than at any other moment in her life.

And she finally felt able to ask for what she wanted from Brian.

She wrenched her mouth free of his marauding lips and thrusting tongue. "Make love to me," Carrie gasped out, too swept away by the sensations cascading through her to be subtle. Emboldened by the desire shining in his eyes, she reached for his belt buckle.

He caught her wrist, startling her.

"What . . ." she began.

"Don't."

All the color drained out of her face. She stared at him, humiliation immediate and devastating. "I don't understand," Carrie managed, even though she suddenly did.

He didn't want her. Why hadn't she seen his reluctance for what it was? She tried to scramble out of his lap.

He stopped her, forcing her to remain perched

atop his powerful thighs, forcing her to allow him to view her humiliation. "You don't understand."

Confused by his rejection, she struggled against his confining hold. "Of course I understand. Despite your behavior the last few days, you've changed your mind."

"I want you, dammit! I want you the way an addict wants a fix. That's not going to change."

She searched his features, wanting to believe him but afraid to. "Why won't you take me, then?" she asked in a small voice.

"It wouldn't be fair to you."

"Fair?" What an odd word, she thought.

"Trust me, it wouldn't be fair. I don't want to hurt you, Carrie. Everyone else in your life has hurt or disappointed you, and I don't want to be another bad experience. You don't deserve that from me."

"You aren't making any sense," she insisted, searching his face, trying to understand.

She suddenly realized that he was deeply troubled about something, and she wondered for a moment if it had anything to do with her. For some inexplicable reason, she doubted it. Her doubt gave her the strength to move beyond her own uncertainty in an effort to help him.

"Brian, tell me what this is all about, because I seriously doubt that this is some misguided attempt at nobility on your part. You want me. I want you."

Lifting his hand, he shoved his fingers through

the thick thatch of hair that capped his head. "I'm making more sense than you could ever possibly know. I'm no good at relationships, Carrie, and you need a real one, a committed relationship with a man who's capable of being a consistent and positive force in your life, someone you can count on."

She felt her heart shift painfully beneath her breasts. "And that isn't what you want? You don't want any kind of a commitment."

"I want a commitment and I want you, but I'm a lousy prospect."

"I don't agree."

He chuckled, the sound mirthless. "Talk to my ex-wife, why don't you? She considers herself quite an authority on the failings of Brian York. I neglect people. I get caught up in my work. In a nutshell, I'm a selfish bastard who always reverts to type. You don't need that kind of aggravation, especially not after what you've been through."

Old baggage from the past, she thought. She knew the weight of old baggage, knew it too well. "I'd rather make my judgments based on what I know about you from personal experience. Who you were in your former marriage has very little to do with who you are now, just as I'm not the woman I was when I was engaged."

Instead of answering her, he reached out to stroke her cheek with his fingertips. The expression on his face spoke of regret.

Carrie turned her face into his hand, her eyes

falling closed as she pressed a kiss into the center of his palm. Although it was a gesture rooted in instinct and desire, she sought nothing more than to reassure him.

When she looked at Brian, she saw his shock. She saw as well the pain that glazed his dark eyes, the same pain she'd glimpsed in the aftermath of the robbery. She knew then that they needed to deal with Brian's past, just as they'd dealt with hers. Otherwise, they didn't have a prayer together.

"Forgive me?" he asked as he carefully drew her forward and embraced her.

She slipped her arms around his neck and pressed a light kiss to his chin. "Always. I care too much about you not to."

Brian exhaled, the sound ragged. "You deserve more than I can offer."

She leaned back, shifting atop his still-aroused body. "How do I stop wanting you?"

"I'll have to keep my hands in my pockets, I guess."

She straightened, smiling gently. She took his hands and brought them to her breasts. Holding them in place against her aching flesh, she felt herself swelling beneath his palms. "I have a better place for them."

His fingers spasmed. He groaned, but he didn't take his hands away. "Carrie . . ."

"I just realized something, Brian York."

"What?" he managed to say through gritted

teeth, his hands forming, shaping her flesh despite the barrier of her clothing.

Smothering a moan of pleasure, she managed to speak. "I know very little about your life before the robbery. I think there are some things I might need to know."

"Like what?"

"Anything," she said, using the same word he'd employed at the bank after he'd been shot. "Everything. What makes you laugh, what makes you sad, and what makes you think you aren't good enough for me."

"That's direct."

"I suspect I need to be right now."

He nodded, but with obvious reluctance.

"Talk to me," she encouraged. "Please."

Carrie brought her hands to his hard cheeks and cupped his face between her palms. Leaning forward, she kissed him with the kind of tenderness that spoke eloquently of her love for him.

She felt Brian's fingers spasm once again, his hold on her growing more and more possessive with every beat of her heart. She arched into his hands without releasing his mouth. Darting her tongue into the dark heat beyond his lips and teeth, Carrie saturated her senses with his taste and drew strength from his ravenous response.

When she eased backward a few minutes later, she said, "Let's talk."

Brian embraced her then, embraced her in such a way that for a moment she feared it might be the last time he ever held her in his arms. His heart thudded violently against her breasts, and when she pressed her lips to the hollow in his throat, she felt the hammering of his pulse.

She told herself not to overreact when he shifted her off his lap and settled her with almost exaggerated care on the couch, as though she might break if he did or said the wrong thing. The troubled expression on his face as he got to his feet and looked down at her assured her that she had cause to worry about his state of mind and her own very vulnerable emotions.

Suddenly chilled, Carrie wrapped her arms around herself and watched him walk to the fireplace. Brian paused at the edge of the hearth, his head bowed. She barely breathed as she waited for him to speak.

"I can't talk about this, Carrie. Not yet, anyway. Not until I've figured out how to handle the situation. I meant it when I said I didn't want to hurt you."

"But, Brian . . ."

He shook his head. "Don't!"

The whiplash sound of his voice stunned and silenced her. It also shattered a large portion of her confidence.

Shocked, she watched him turn away and stride out of the cabin. He didn't return until well after she'd climbed into bed that night.

The next thirty-six hours passed at a snail's pace. They ate their meals together, but without conversation. Neither one spoke when it came time to go to bed.

Carrie took periodic walks with the FBI field agent. She also tried to lose herself in the book she'd brought with her, but the endeavor proved futile. She couldn't concentrate on the text for more than a few minutes at a time.

She watched Brian grow more restless and edgy. He prowled the interior of the cabin until she wanted to scream. He spoke only when spoken to, his responses monosyllabic.

Carrie finally drew an obvious and very painful conclusion. In spite of his initial attraction to her and all his words to the contrary, Brian had reevaluated his feelings and decided that he didn't want her after all.

Being so honest with herself hurt, but Carrie didn't know how else to deal with his rejection, especially if she expected to recover from it.

Carrie Forbes intended to make a full recovery. She silently and repeatedly promised herself that she would—and she always kept her promises.

NINE

Brian grabbed the kitchen wall phone before it rang a second time. He barked a greeting, then listened intently to the caller on the other end of the line.

Standing a few feet away, Carrie reached for the coffeepot, which she'd washed and placed in the dish rack a few moments earlier. Barefoot and clad in a cropped white tee and matching shorts, she concentrated on drying the pot as her gaze strayed to Brian's face.

He looked exhausted and tense—which was just the way she felt, and probably looked, for that matter. She sighed, the sound replete with sadness and regret for what might have been between them.

She knew she needed to get back to her home and to her life. She told herself that being alone was preferable to being with a man who barely tolerated her existence, but the lie felt like what it was. A lie. She wanted him so badly that she ached. Everywhere. Constantly.

Even though she still trusted Brian to behave protectively if her safety was threatened, she loathed being trapped in the cabin with him. He clearly hated it as well.

"What kind of a timetable are we looking at?" he finally asked the caller.

Although Carrie didn't understand the direction of the conversation, she concluded that this was their usual morning telephone call from Detective Landis. No one else knew how to reach them. She felt the fatigue of yet another sleepless night, not just the distance that Brian had chosen to put between them, weigh her down as she set aside the dish towel.

Intent on placing the pot in the coffeemaker, she stepped away from the sink, but she hesitated halfway to the counter on the opposite side of the kitchen when she heard Brian hang up the phone.

Carrie glanced over her shoulder. "Have they made any progress?"

He met her gaze, his expression brooding. "They picked them up this morning."

She felt the shock of his announcement slam into her. The coffeepot slipped from her suddenly nerveless fingers, the glass exploding like a grenade when it hit the kitchen tile.

"The other two are in custody?" she whispered. Frozen in place, she didn't quite believe what Brian had just told her.

He jerked a nod in her direction, his gaze flashing down to the floor and then back up to her face. "Don't move," he ordered.

She frowned, still feeling disoriented. "Quit telling me what to do."

It was over. They were over. Life would go on. She didn't know whether to laugh or to cry.

"Don't move, Carrie," he said again, ignoring her.

Defiance and a thousand conflicting emotions rose up inside her. She didn't think. She simply began to take a step, but she didn't get a chance to complete it.

Brian surged in her direction and grabbed her. Glass crunched beneath his shoes as he scooped her off her feet.

Carrie was beyond hearing the sound of crushed glass. Something unraveled within her when he touched her, something fragile. She felt his strength, and all the control she'd exerted over herself during the previous thirty-six hours went up in flames.

"Damn you!" she shouted, struggling to free herself.

He muttered an answering curse, but it sounded more like a verbal caress as he brought her against his chest.

Carrie gripped his shoulders. "Put me down this instant. I'm not a sack of potatoes."

He backed out of the kitchen, strain in his hard-featured face as she twisted her body against him in order to free herself.

Her breasts throbbed. She shuddered, then renewed her effort to free herself.

"There's glass all over the floor," he reminded her tersely.

"I know that," she insisted, trying to wedge her arm between her breasts and his chest.

"You're not wearing any shoes."

She stopped struggling and stared at him, then sagged in his arms. How stupid! A sob rooted in rejection and embarrassment rippled through her.

"Carrie."

She heard a wealth of emotion in his voice, but none of it made any sense to her. Why, she wondered, did life have to be so blasted complicated all of the time? Why couldn't she have what she wanted? Just this one time.

"Are you all right?"

She pushed at the lock of auburn hair that had fallen across her temple. "I'm fine, and I'm sorry. I was just so shocked by the news."

"You don't have to explain."

Still clasped against his chest, she felt the furious pounding of his heart. The vibrations sank into her and mated with her own racing heart. She saw as well the ruddy color that stained his cheeks. She knew then that he wasn't as immune to her as he would have her believe.

"This entire situation has turned me into a deranged woman, and I hate it."

"Hate me," he suggested. "I probably caused it."

"I don't hate you," she whispered as she stared at him. "I don't, Brian." *I love you,* she thought, *and it's breaking my heart.*

He clenched his jaws for a long moment, then exhaled heavily. "You should."

She shook her head, the tears swelling in her throat and stinging her eyes making it impossible to speak. Despite her desire not to humiliate herself any further, a single tear slipped down her cheek.

"I need you," he said, his voice so hoarse that she strained to hear his words.

She understood his meaning, though, and she felt the wall she'd constructed around her emotions crumble to dust. Just once, she told herself. Just this once. *Dear God, I need him so much. I need to feel. I've been so cold and so alone for so long.*

"I need you too," Carrie said.

Desire darkened his eyes, turning them into bottomless pools of obsidian. "Are you saying yes?"

She nodded.

"Why?"

She placed her fingertips against his lips. "No more questions, Brian, because I haven't got any answers left."

He lowered her to stand between his muscular

thighs. Bringing her hand back up to his lips, he pressed a kiss to the tip of each finger before shifting his attention to the center of her palm.

She felt the sweep of his tongue, then the delicate ribbons of sensations that stole into her bloodstream. She quivered, not with any kind of trepidation, but with anticipation.

She hid nothing as she stared up at him. How could she? Carrie wondered. She knew that love shouldn't ever be concealed under a barrel or secreted in a closet. She'd had precious little of the emotion in her life, and she desperately needed to express what she felt for him, even if she didn't receive the same gift in return.

She loved Brian, loved him with every breath she took and with every beat of her heart. She would give that love now, without conditions and without restraint.

Brian lifted her into his arms and carried her the short distance to her bedroom. Placing her on the bed, he dropped down beside her and drew her into the glorious heat of his body.

"Do you trust me?" he asked.

She blinked in surprise. "Of course."

"And you know that whatever happens between us, you're in control, and that I'll stop if you ask me to? Whenever you ask me."

She nodded, because she believed him. While she appreciated his sensitivity, she wanted to be normal, to feel normal. She wanted that more than anything.

"Take me . . ." she began, then paused as she searched for the right way to say what she meant.

"Where, Carrie?" he encouraged as he gathered her into his arms. "You want me to take you where?"

"Take me beyond control. Please take me there. I've waited so long, and I can't wait any longer."

He smiled, but he didn't waste a moment teasing her about her good manners. He took her lips then, gently, tenderly, as though they had all the time in the world to indulge themselves.

She arched into him, her breasts flattening against the hard wall of his chest as she slipped her arms around his neck. Parting her lips, she nibbled at his lower lip, then sucked at the tip of his tongue. She invited. She teased. And without realizing it, she seduced, innocently and thoroughly.

Brian taught her erotic lessons about kissing. She followed where he led, delighting in the various textures and tastes of his passion until she felt intoxicated by their endless, hot, openmouthed kiss—a kiss that imitated the ultimate intimacy and nearly drove her to the brink of madness.

He drew her up until she sat astride him, her thighs overlapping his, their loins not quite touching. She imagined then what it would be like between them when their bodies were finally joined, and she felt her insides spasm with anticipation.

His gaze riveted on her flushed features, Brian removed his shirt, then lifted her T-shirt over her head and tossed it aside. Carrie held her breath, the impulse to cover her naked breasts eclipsed by the approval she saw shining in his eyes. Her nipples tightened under his gaze. She trembled, and the air trapped in her chest exited her body in a rush when he leaned down.

He circled each delicate, mauve-colored tip with his tongue, painting a moist trail of scorching heat across her flesh. Then he used his teeth on her, carefully and very deliberately. Evocative sensations turned to ribbons of flame inside her, licking at her soul and threatening to incinerate her.

Carrie clutched at Brian's shoulders to steady herself. Because he still hadn't actually put his hands on her, her breasts swelled as if to beg for his touch. She arched her back like an exotic feline, her body speaking for her. She heard his indrawn breath, and she felt the tension vibrating throughout him.

The soft, inarticulate sounds she made as he suckled her filled the air, sounds borne in her heart, sounds that begged him never to stop this delicious torture. When he raised his head to look at her, she felt the impact of his dark-eyed gaze reverberate through her entire body.

His name spilled past her lips, part plea, part question. He smiled, reclaiming her mouth as he took her hands. As they faced each other he joined their palms, then meshed his fingers with her more slender ones.

Lips fused and hands mated, they lingered and sipped from each other.

They played an erotic game of their own design, tongues darting and dueling, palms still joined, the pressure and heat of their connection sending wave after wave of desire undulating into Carrie's veins.

Sensual messages flooded her mind. Her senses glittered like fireworks on the Fourth of July. She felt her heart swell with emotion, until she thought her body might not be able to contain it much longer.

Moaning softly, she shimmied forward so that her breasts brushed against Brian. She felt her nipples pucker to aching points of need each time she swayed against the dense pelt of hair that covered his muscled chest.

Brian groaned at the contact, the sound coming from deep inside him. He gripped her hands. She knew the instant his control began to slip. She felt and tasted his ravenous appetite as he ate at her like a man starved for sustenance. In the privacy of her mind, she savored the knowledge that she alone would be the one to appease his desire.

Carrie felt utterly sensitized, as though transformed into some priceless instrument of pleasure that a virtuoso would select for himself. Despite the unsettling newness of the experience, she surrendered without hesitation to the feelings coursing through her body and the emotions filling her heart.

Whatever happened between them, she knew she wouldn't ever regret this time with Brian.

Brian released her lips a few moments later.

Carrie gasped for breath.

"Talk to me," he urged. "Tell me what you're feeling right now."

She heard the rawness in his voice, and knew it echoed her own. "Everything," she confessed.

"I want to give you everything," Brian said.

"Touch me," she whispered.

"Tell me where."

"Everywhere."

"No boundaries?" he asked.

As she looked at him Carrie realized that his tense expression was a product of both restraint and desire. Feeling bolder than she'd ever felt before, she reached down and smoothed a fingertip over his swollen sex, then dragged her knuckles up his flat belly. He jerked under her touch, his body, although shielded by coarse denim, more responsive than she'd ever imagined it might be.

She smiled, adoring the uneven cadence of his breathing, not just savoring the fact that she was capable of seduction. She felt a rush of pure feminine power hit her bloodstream like a potent drug.

"No boundaries, Brian. No limits or rules. I want it all with you."

He shuddered. "So do I. My God, so do I."

She stared at him. His features all harsh angles and lines, his eyes burned with an intensity that should have terrified her. But it didn't, no more than he did.

Her gaze never leaving his face, Carrie shifted her body until she was reclining against a mound of pillows. She caught his hands. A slight tug, and Brian followed her down to the sheet-covered mattress. He stretched out beside her, rather than subjecting her to the weight of his large body.

Unable to bear the fabric that separated them, she placed her hand over his and guided it to the waistband of her shorts. She sensed from the expression on his face that he understood her frustration with the barrier.

He proved it a moment later when he helped her shed what remained of her clothing, although not his own. She wondered why, but he quickly displaced her curiosity.

Brian started slowly, cupping her full breasts, teasing the nipples with his fingers until she almost begged for his mouth. She quivered as he explored her, her eyes never leaving his face.

He mapped her contours and curves with a thoroughness that left her breathless and writhing atop the mattress. He measured every aspect of her hourglass-shaped body with knowledgeable hands, as though to memorize her narrow waist, the soft curve of her stomach, and the feminine width of her hips.

She moaned his name when he moved lower and combed his fingers through the auburn silk that shielded her secrets. Stirring restlessly, she unconsciously parted her legs, her message clear even if unstated.

Carrie felt empty inside, and she wanted him to fill her. Wanted, needed to feel him throbbing deep inside her body. She wanted that feeling more than she'd ever wanted anything in her entire life.

Brian responded to her unvoiced need. He curved his hand over her, his hold on her more possessive than anything she'd ever experienced. When he dipped two fingers into the snug, damp channel that would eventually embrace his sex, Carrie quaked with sensation—shocking sensations that she'd never known before.

Leaning over her, Brian took her lips while simultaneously stoking the flames within her into a firestorm. Her hips lifted up from the bed, seeking, searching for more. Much more.

She felt a quickening deep within and cried out, twining her arms around his neck. She bucked under his touch, twisting wildly against the pressure of his hands and fingers. A sudden cloudburst of sizzling inner rain saturated her senses and intensified the already feverish passion of her journey to completion.

He kept stroking her, his touch the closest thing to heaven she'd ever known. Spiraling sensations tightened like a vise inside her. She pushed against his hand and gasped his name, over and over again, blindly seeking release from the pressure building inside her lower body. It threatened to send her over the edge at any moment, but she didn't fear the sweet madness that seemed intent on enveloping her.

It finally did when Brian accelerated his penetration of her body and simultaneously sucked a taut nipple into his mouth.

Her climax happened suddenly, almost like a bolt of hot summer lightning across a night sky.

Carrie screamed Brian's name, her mind and body liberated from the emotional wasteland of the past and launched into a new world. She went spinning out of control, thoroughly caught up in the convulsive shudders rocking her body and numbing her mind to everything but the feelings sweeping her into a sensory heaven.

Brian reclaimed her mouth once again, inhaling the shocked sounds she made while she unraveled in the storm he'd created for her. After a while, when the quaking of her body eased and her stunned cries abated, he soothed her with gentle hands and light kisses.

Her breathing still uneven, Carrie sagged in his embrace. Aftershocks tremored through her, and his sensual generosity moved her to tears. She wept, unable to stop herself from expressing the emotion she felt.

"It was your first one," he said. Positioned on his side, he cradled her against his chest and stroked her from shoulder to hip.

A latent sob slipped free. She could barely think, so she simply nodded.

Easing her backward Brian looked down at her, his expression tender as he wiped away the tears staining her flushed cheeks.

"My first," she managed, still marveling over the intensity of her release.

"I'm glad it was with me."

Her chin wobbled. "So am I."

The utterly profound need that she felt to mate with Brian beckoned to Carrie in the minutes that followed. It fueled as well the courage she'd so recently acquired where he was concerned.

She tugged his head down so that she could kiss him, this time the one to stake her claim, this time the one who would explore and taunt and tantalize. She trusted instinct and desire then, unaware of the seductive quality of her innocence.

She bathed his lower lip with the tip of her tongue, then applied gentle teeth to the same expanse. Brian groaned, his hand curving over the back of her neck.

Laughing softly, Carrie brushed his hand aside, her message clear. This was her adventure, at least for the moment, and she expected him to cooperate.

He gripped the bedding, his hands fisting when she deepened their kiss. His taste, so darkly sensual, entranced and fascinated her. She lingered at his mouth, indulging her senses with evocative forays that made Brian moan his pleasure.

After skimming her hands across his shoulders and down his back, she brought them to the front of his body and reached for the button at the waistband of his jeans. She paused, though, and met his gaze when she felt the stillness that settled over Brian.

"You're sure?" he asked, cupping her cheek in his hand.

She smiled, smoothing her fingertips across the ridge of flesh still concealed by his clothing. She felt the pulsing power of his body, and longed to have it buried inside her.

He sucked in a harsh breath. "Carrie?"

"I've never been more sure of anything in my entire life."

He nodded, then planted a hard little kiss on her lips.

Carrie freed the button and lowered the zipper.

His eyes never leaving her face, Brian separated their bodies for the brief moments that it took to shed his jeans and briefs.

Once he settled back on the bed, he brought her into his arms. His arousal pressed against her lower abdomen, the heat and hardness of his flesh branding her.

She pressed a string of kisses along his jaw. "I want to touch you the way you touched me."

"Are you afraid?" he asked in a low voice.

"I've never been afraid of you, or of sharing this with you."

"I want it to be right for you, Carrie."

"It is," she vowed as she nudged him onto his back, knelt beside him, and stroked him from hip to shoulder. "Nothing in my life has ever been more right."

His eyes fell closed, and he shook beneath her fingers as she trailed them over his muscular anatomy. The evidence of his desire drew her attention, and she responded to the summons. She reached for him then, her inner temperature rising several degrees as she clasped his hard length between her hands and caressed him.

Brian shuddered and uttered a guttural sound, part pain, part pleasure.

Too eager to know every powerful inch of the body of the man she would love until she drew her last breath, she lost touch with reality and focused on her driving need to pleasure him. Words of love rushed from her mind to her lips, but she bit them back. Although she experienced a momentary twinge of sadness, she sensed that this wasn't the time to express aloud the depth of her feelings for Brian. She didn't want him to feel obligated or trapped, and she feared damaging the moment.

Giving of herself would have to suffice, she decided, at least for now.

She touched him everywhere, an unexpected greed bursting to life inside her as her hands roamed over his body. She returned again and again to his jutting maleness, delighting in the tremors of response that rocked him each time she stroked him. Corresponding tremors rippled through her from head to toe.

She knew she shocked him when she lowered her head to his abdomen and trailed her tongue across the muscular expanse. She took her time, the tension and heat building inside her as seductive as the tense heat radiating from Brian's rigid body. She hesitated for a moment, then indulged a sudden sensual impulse that she'd never before experienced.

She took him into her mouth, tentatively at first, then with kind of confidence that only love can inspire. His breathing stopped for a long moment, then resumed on a groan that seemed to go on forever. She understood his surprise, because she'd surprised herself with her desire to know him this way, this soon.

She sensed the self-control he exerted over himself as he gave her the time she needed to make this erotic journey. She sensed as well his willingness to make himself vulnerable, despite the test to his nerves, as he granted her the freedom to discover him and to learn her power over him, not just the fact that boundary lines and the anxiety of inexperience disappeared completely when lovers truly trusted each other.

He whispered her name, the sound as it emerged from him very nearly like a prayer. Lifting her head, she met his gaze. The stark expression on his face made her feel as though she'd just been given a glimpse of the secrets hidden in the depths of his soul.

She flowed up his body, instinct her guide yet again as she positioned herself over him. He bracketed her hips with his hands, holding her poised above him.

"I need to protect you," he reminded her in a voice that sounded like he'd just run ten miles.

"I'm safe," she gasped out, referring to the birth-control method she used despite the absence of intimacy in her life. "My monthly cycle needed to be regulated."

Brian nodded. "You don't need to worry about my health."

"I know that." And she did. Life was complicated these days, but Brian was the last man in the world who would knowingly jeopardize her.

He lowered her hips then.

Carrie trembled when she felt the swollen head of his sex at the entrance of her body. "I need you," she said, her body so hungry for his that she felt desire vibrate deep inside her. "I need you so much I feel like I'm dying from it."

He drove his hips upward, penetrating her slick, swollen depths until she shuddered around him, accustoming herself to the feel of him within the snug confines of a body untouched for so many years. He held very still, perspiration sheening his tanned skin, the muscles beneath vibrating with his restraint. And once again he whispered her name in that reverent tone of voice that made her heart expand with emotions still unspoken.

Bracing herself with her hands on his chest, Carrie moved, experimentally at first, then with greater confidence and intent. She undulated like a willow captured by a sultry summer breeze, her eyes falling closed, her breathing labored, her body clutching his flesh in a seductive fist of heat and humidity that sent waves of sensation flowing outward until they consumed her. She felt drenched in a fire-tinged rain, and she succumbed willingly to her certainty that she would soon drown in the downpour.

Brian exercised every ounce of control he possessed in the ensuing minutes, despite the fact that his entire body felt like dynamite about to detonate.

He let Carrie set their pace, which increased in concert with her confidence as she rode him and tested his endurance. She leaned forward, her back arching and her breasts plumping against his chest as she sought his mouth. Tiny sounds escaped her, sounds that incited and provoked and thoroughly jeopardized his control. He drank them in, though, tasting her passion, savoring it, submerging himself in it until he didn't know where his body stopped and hers began.

He tightened his hold on her hips, his fingers digging into her. A harsh sound erupted from him. He surged upward, repeatedly, his heartbeat a deafening roar in his ears, the blood pounding through his veins like a rampaging river at flood-stage.

Seconds later Brian felt the change in her body and heard the breathless pleas that reflected her quest for completion. His own body simultaneously demanded release.

They slammed together with tempered violence, their mating more than a union of bodies, but one of souls and hearts.

Carrie cried out suddenly, her insides quivering and clutching at his engorged flesh until he thought he might go insane. He heard her gasp his name, a stunned sound that preceded the tumult that claimed her.

He felt the force of her climax, felt it suck them both into a whirlpool of pure sensation that effectively demolished his control once and for all.

Brian answered her cry with one of his own. He willingly surrendered to the erotic fire of the woman writhing atop him. As her body milked a sustained climax from him, he struggled for breath and grappled with the realization that he'd finally found his true mate.

Carrie eventually slumped forward across his chest with a shattered sigh. When she tucked her face against his neck and wrapped her arms around him, Brian embraced her, cherishing the woman and what they'd just shared.

TEN

The following morning Carrie finished collecting the last of her toiletries from the bathroom and tucked them into her overnight bag. Walking back into her bedroom, she paused at the end of the bed and dropped the small bag into her suitcase.

As she closed the piece of luggage and locked it, her memories of the preceding twenty-four hours flooded her mind and caused emotions she couldn't control to sting her eyes. She swallowed, trying to ease the thickness in her throat as she allowed her gaze to drift over the now-stripped mattress before moving on to the blankets and pillows stacked neatly in a nearby chair.

The room looked like it had when she and Brian had first arrived at the cabin, but appearances were deceiving. Carrie Forbes knew far too much about appearances ever to be fooled by them.

Illusion versus reality. She'd had the latter used against her in the past in order to produce the former, and she'd learned in the intervening years how to reverse the process.

Brian had changed her view of the world and of herself, though. Nothing in her life would ever be the same, she reflected. Nothing. She knew that fact as well as she knew her own name.

Carrie pressed her palms together, badly shaken by the uncertainty and self-doubt reemerging within her. Despite her best efforts, she couldn't find a way to discard the melancholy feeling that had plagued her since getting out of bed that morning.

Because she'd lingered in the shower and then made only a brief appearance in the kitchen for coffee, rather than joining Brian at the breakfast table, she couldn't pretend that he wasn't aware of her withdrawal. She was grateful that he hadn't pressed her for an explanation, but she realized that he eventually would.

Carrie hated the idea of explaining her state of mind, because she didn't completely understand it yet herself. A door slammed somewhere in the cabin, jarring her from her thoughts. She glanced at her watch. She had only a few minutes left to pull herself together for the drive home.

Back to the world.

Back to reality.

The memories they'd made there, in the cabin and in this bed, would stay with her forever, she knew. A source of private joy, but also, she feared, a reminder of what she seriously doubted she would ever be able to claim as her own—not because of Brian but because of her own inadequacies.

Carrie sank down onto the edge of the bed; the achiness in her body from the stunning, pulse-pounding intimacy they'd shared and the emotions still threatening her composure added reminders of the time she'd spent in Brian's arms.

She couldn't *not* think about this man who embodied her secret hopes and dreams. He dominated her thoughts, whether or not he was close at hand. A sensual and generous lover, Brian had given her the opportunity to discover a side of herself she hadn't even known existed.

Where had all that inner fire come from? she wondered, still amazed by the freedom and passion she'd found with him.

She trembled, recalling her shattered cries of pleasure, her disbelief, and her desire to drive him beyond the control he'd exercised over himself in order to indulge her senses and help her reclaim her sexual confidence.

She took pride in the fact that she'd succeeded in pushing him past his restraint. The experience had been a revelation and more empowering than she would ever have believed possible.

The breathtakingly erotic hours they'd shared were etched into her memory. Brian had opened her eyes to all that she'd missed over the years, to the woman hidden within, and to what she would lose if she walked away from him.

In truth, Carrie hardly recognized the sensuous creature she'd become during their lovemaking. She didn't know how to deal with that woman. Was she a temporary visitor? Or would she linger and blossom even more? The possibility of the latter intrigued and tempted her, but another possibility existed and it lurked like a dark specter in her heart. What if that newly discovered woman disappeared? She wondered as well if she was even capable of sustaining a relationship with a vital, sexy man like Brian.

He'd thoroughly turned her world upside down. Add that to the unbalancing impact of the robbery and their subsequent decision to use Landis's mountain cabin as a safehouse until the robbers were apprehended, and it was no wonder she felt confused. She just wished she didn't.

She loved Brian, loved him so deeply that her feelings unnerved her. Carrie feared failing herself and him if they continued to see each other. She feared failure in the same way that most people feared death. She also feared hurting him.

Despite his sturdy exterior and strong personality, she'd had glimpses of Brian's vulnerability. She knew he wasn't made of stone or steel. He was a man who'd doubted himself when his marriage had failed, yet he'd been sensitive enough to question whether or not he could meet her emotional needs, not simply satisfy her physical desires.

Carrie covered her face with her hands, struggling for an inner calm that would allow her to get through the long drive home with Brian, not just the responsibilities that awaited them at police headquarters.

Later, Carrie promised herself as she got up from the bed and reached for her suitcase, she would regain some kind of rational perspective and confront her own emotions. She knew she owed herself and Brian the effort. She just hoped that he'd give her the time she needed.

"What's wrong?"

Carrie stiffened briefly before she answered him. "Nothing's wrong." Handing her suitcase to Brian as they stood beside the open trunk of his car, she asked, "Do we have everything?"

"Everything but you," he remarked as he placed her luggage in the trunk and worked at containing his growing uneasiness.

Carrie darted a glance in his direction, but her expression remained closed. "I'll check inside one more time, just to be sure."

Brian watched her make her way to the front door of the cabin. Once she disappeared from sight, he slammed the trunk lid, swore, and then told himself to settle down.

His common sense insisted that Carrie deserved a chance to come to terms with all the changes that had taken place between them, but he felt her pulling away from him. Her behavior gnawed on his nerves.

He reminded himself that the years of self-doubt she'd experienced couldn't be healed overnight. He also knew that he needed to exercise patience with her, something he rarely managed to do under the best of circumstances with anyone.

His emotions were exposed, raw, and he didn't like the way he felt. He was a man who prided himself on total control of his world, but he knew in his gut that he had no right to place demands on or try to control Carrie. If he did either one of those things, she would run for the nearest exit.

Individually, they had issues—what Carrie had called baggage from the past—to deal with. Together or apart, neither one could afford to ignore those issues, but knowing didn't make it any easier to digest or accept. Brian swore again, this time the curse more vicious sounding than the first.

He hoped that the tough day ahead of them was a part of her preoccupation. He'd told her that Landis expected them at police headquarters for another lineup once they returned to San Diego, and the district attorney's office wanted to interview them as well.

As he waited for Carrie to finish her inspection of the cabin, Brian knew he was kidding himself. He suspected that what bothered her had everything to do with a day and night of lovemaking, not with the justice system.

He also sensed that she now regretted what they'd shared, although he didn't understand why. He planned to, though. She was the most innately sensual woman he'd ever known, which he considered something of a miracle given her past, but a miracle he was grateful for, nonetheless. She was also the most honest and instinctively loving person he'd ever encountered. No hidden agendas, no game playing, unlike his ex-wife, who'd excelled in those arenas when she'd wanted something.

Somehow, Brian promised himself, they would deal with Carrie's concerns once she revealed them, and somehow he'd convince her that they belonged together. He knew, even if she didn't, that the chemistry between them was as unique as the bond of trust forged during their first moments together on the floor of the bank. He wasn't about to give up on her without a fight. Hell! He'd conduct a war, if that's what it took to persuade her not to run from the first genuine happiness either one of them had ever known.

He wanted her as much as he wanted to live, and he intended to have her. Failure wasn't an acceptable outcome where Carrie was concerned.

Brian watched her step out of the cabin, pull the door closed behind her, lock it, and then tuck the key into the pocket of her slacks. Her expression still unrevealing, she walked toward him.

"We're all set," she told him as she neared the car.

He caught her hand as she started to sidestep him. "I don't think so."

She looked at him, wariness in her eyes as she kept her gaze steady.

"How about a hug?"

"Sure." She stepped forward and gave him a perfunctory squeeze.

He stopped her when she tried to shift out of reach. "What was that?"

"A hug."

"I don't think so," he said quietly. "It didn't feel quite right."

"Why?"

"It just didn't. Care to try again?" he asked, although he didn't wait for her reply. He drew her into his arms, mourned the stiffness of her body, then felt his heart sink when she didn't relax her posture at all in the moments that followed.

"We need to leave," Carrie said.

"We need a lot of things," Brian remarked, his hands gliding up and down her back, his tight jaw reflecting the emotional stress he felt. "Time. Privacy. Quiet conversations. Long walks on the beach. Slow dancing. Good food. Beautiful sunsets. Lots of things ahead, if you're brave enough to take a chance on us."

She stared at his chest. "This isn't . . . Brian, please don't start anything now. We don't have the time."

He placed a fingertip beneath her chin, nudging her face into view. "Trust me, Carrie."

She glanced away. "I do."

"What happened between us wasn't a mistake."

Exhaling softly, she asked, "How can you be so sure?"

He gathered her against his chest, needing to feel her softness as he inhaled the fragrance that would forever intoxicate his senses. He silently willed her to slide her arms around his waist, but she didn't. Regretfully, he released her.

"How, Brian?"

"I just am."

She stiffened and shook her head, clearly not willing to debate the subject with him.

"What are you afraid of?" he asked, not altogether certain he wanted to hear her answer but aware that he needed to if he was going to deal with what troubled her.

She pressed her fingertips to her temple. "We should be going now. We don't want to be late for our appointment with Detective Landis."

"He'll wait," Brian ground out, his temper flaring. "He doesn't have a case without us."

Her hand drifted down to her side, and she squared her shoulders, her determination apparent as she glared at him. "I want to leave, Brian. Now, please."

Although thoroughly frustrated, he found the strength to contain his unraveling temper, turned, and yanked open the passenger-side door. He strode to the driver's side, got into the vehicle, and started the engine.

Brian didn't speak again until he guided the car into the parking lot of police headquarters several hours later. Neither did Carrie.

Clutching her purse in one hand, she reached for the door handle with the other. Brian turned off the ignition, leaned across her, and stopped her from shoving open the door by placing his hand atop hers.

Wariness sparked to life in her eyes again as she met his gaze.

He gave her a piercing look. "There's something I want to tell you, if you're willing to listen."

Carrie nodded with obvious reluctance, sank back in the bucket seat, and folded her hands atop her lap.

Brian spoke with his usual candor. "When my marriage crashed and burned, I promised myself that I'd never get entangled emotionally with another woman. Gloria did a good job of convincing me that I was a self-absorbed bastard with little regard for the emotional needs of other people. In particular, her needs. She gave me a laundry list of my failings as a husband, and it really shook my confidence about my ability to hold up my end of things in a committed relationship. I couldn't, and still can't, for that matter, fault her, because she wasn't wrong. I'd spent most of our years together focused on work, what she referred to as 'empire building.' I liked the image, because I'd started out with virtually nothing but my determination to make a success of my life. We drifted apart. It happened slowly, and I didn't give it much thought, to be quite honest. I was busy. She had her social activities and her charities. She didn't want children, and I didn't press her. She seemed happy with our life. At least I assumed she was because it was like the world she'd grown up in, but that was my mistake." He paused, taking a moment to assemble the rest of his thoughts.

"You don't have to do this," Carrie said. "I know it has to be difficult for you."

He shook his head. "I probably would have agreed with you a few weeks ago, but I don't now. Too much is at stake. I was thinking about my relationship with Gloria during the drive back, and I realized that we always had great sex, but we never really made love. It's strange, but I didn't realize that fact until you and I had been together, nor did I realize that it makes a difference to me now."

Carrie stared at him, shock in her pale features and wide eyes.

Brian exhaled, the sound weighted with too many emotions to express at that moment and a large amount of frustration. "We went through the motions of being a couple, but we were pretty indifferent to each other after the first few years of our marriage. We rarely talked or exchanged confidences. Our marriage can be described in one word—superficial. I regret that now, but I can't change what happened between us. Anyway, the few relationships I had right after the divorce were short-term and mostly physical, but they left a bitter taste in my mouth after a while, so I stopped bothering. Until you," he admitted, the truth hard to say but necessary, if he had a prayer of reaching her and salvaging what they'd begun at the cabin. "Until you, Carrie."

"Why are you telling me all this?"

He felt more emotionally naked than at any other time in his adult life, but he knew there was no going back now. The realization that he was falling in love with her had nearly poleaxed him during the silent drive from the cabin. The added realization that he was about to lose her clinched his decision to forge ahead now. "I'm no prize, and I know it."

"You've obviously changed," she observed, reaching out to him.

He gripped her hand. "I'd like to think I have, but I suspect the real test is ahead."

"You're a very giving and loving man, Brian York, and you'll never convince me otherwise, even though you're bossy to a fault some of the time," she said gently. "The problem we're having right now is with me, not you, so don't beat yourself up over something you can't control or manage."

He hesitated for a moment, carefully weighing his next remark. Rather than bombard her with his newly discovered feelings for her and risk scaring her off, he tempered his next statement even though it went against the grain of his blunt personality. "You matter to me, Carrie. You matter a hell of a lot more than I thought anyone ever could, but you're pulling away from me. I don't like it, and I think I deserve to know the reason why."

Her eyes filled with tears. She withdrew her hand and dug around in her purse for a tissue. After blotting her cheeks, she said, "I'm sorry, but I can't talk about it yet."

He nodded, his jaw tightening with the control he exerted over himself. "Will you ever?"

She worried her lower lip with her front teeth before looking at him. "I honestly don't know."

He studied her then, studied her for several moments during which the only sound in the interior of the car was the ticking of the dashboard clock.

"We'd better go inside now," Carrie finally said as she reached for the door handle. "Detective Landis will send out a search party if we keep him waiting much longer."

Landis met them at the elevator. Clearly annoyed with how late they were, although he didn't say a single critical word when he noted the strained condition of his two prime witnesses, he escorted them to his office.

"We're poised to do the lineups in about fifteen minutes. Can I assume that you're both still in this game to win?"

Carrie nodded.

"We're committed. Who goes first?" Brian asked.

"Let's have Ms. Forbes do the two lineups while the assistant district attorney interviews you, Mr. York. In fact, Joe Kelsey is waiting for you in the conference room at the end of the hall right now. I'll stay with Ms. Forbes until Kelsey's ready to speak to her, then we'll reverse the process."

"Sounds good," Brian observed.

"I'm ready, if you are," Carrie said to the detective.

Brian snagged her wrist before she could follow Landis out of his office and into the hallway. "I'll take you home when we're finished."

"All right," she said, looking up at him. "Good luck. Don't forget to tell Mr. Kelsey that we didn't discuss the robbery while we were out of town. He'll want to know."

He admired her clearheadedness, but he couldn't ignore the anxiety shadowing her eyes. Brian gently tugged her forward.

Carrie walked straight into his embrace.

A little shocked but relieved by her spontaneous response, Brian didn't question his good fortune. He closed his arms around her, nearly groaning aloud as his body reacted to the feel of her full breasts against his chest and the perfect fit of her hips to his loins.

He heard the ragged sigh that escaped her, and it served to clear his senses and reinforce his concern for her. He belatedly felt her gathering her strength in order to face the emotional rigors of two more lineups. Although worried about the future of their relationship—if they had a future at all, he silently amended—he felt mounting concern for Carrie's well-being at that moment.

She stepped back before he could voice his thoughts. "How is it that you always seem to know when I need a hug?"

Smiling faintly, she didn't wait for his reply. She turned away and joined Landis, who glanced at Brian, then nodded.

He silently applauded the detective for keeping his surprise under control and his opinions to himself even though he'd observed their exchange. Brian watched Carrie until she turned a corner at the end of the hallway with Landis and disappeared from sight. He then made his way to the conference room at the opposite end of the hall.

The lineups and preliminary interviews took almost five hours. Brian waited for Carrie in the visitors' lounge they'd used during their first meeting with Landis. He drove her to her home as dusk settled over the California coastline.

A few blocks from her neighborhood, he

asked, "How about some takeout for supper? I've discovered a great Chinese place in Del Mar that delivers."

She shook her head. "I'm too tired to bother with food right now. All I really want is a hot shower and a decent night of sleep."

He pulled into her driveway a few minutes later. "Go ahead inside while I get your things out of the trunk."

She did as he suggested. He saw her weariness in every step she took to her front door. After depositing her luggage in the entryway, Brian found her in the kitchen.

"Why don't I stay the night with you?"

Carrie raised startled eyes to his face, the mail she'd been sorting forgotten in the wake of his suggestion. "That's not a good idea right now."

"Don't do this to us," he urged, his voice level, his expression like carved granite.

"I need some time to myself."

He felt his anger ignite and rush like fire into his veins. It flared out of control, much like the end result of a match being dropped into a river of gasoline. "Talk to me, dammit! I can't stand this."

Carrie's fury matched Brian's explosive temper. "Don't you dare try to bully me into submission. I don't owe you or anyone else explanations on demand, so get that notion out of your head right this minute."

"Make an exception," he insisted as he approached her and curved his hands over her shoulders.

She stood her ground, the strength of her character evident in her flashing eyes and posture. "I know you've had a miserable day. So have I, but try to understand. I want to be left alone. I . . . want . . . my . . . privacy," she enunciated with exaggerated care, "and I expect you to back up and give it to me, because if you keep prodding me, I won't have anything to say to you. Not ever. Do you understand what I'm telling you?"

"I understand completely," he said, his voice as sharp as a blade.

Carrie shook her head as she shrugged free of his hands. "No, Brian, I don't think you do. With a little luck, though, you might actually want to understand when you calm down. Right now, all you want to do is manage me into submission. It will not happen, so stop trying. I honestly don't know if I can sustain a relationship with any man, and I need to work this through on my own. Are you satisfied? Now you know what's troubling me, so please leave. I don't have anything left to say to you tonight."

Incredulous, he asked, "Is this about sex?"

"Brian . . ." she began, her exasperation with him more than a little obvious.

"Is it?" he demanded.

"Sex is a secondary issue, but it's an issue."

"I don't believe this. Didn't yesterday and last night prove anything to you about yourself?"

She lifted her chin. "I don't want to fail."

"Pride," he bit out. "This is about your pride, isn't it?"

She exhaled a shuddery-sounding rush of air. "Try self-preservation, not pride."

"You're wrong. This has everything to do with pride and cowardice, and you know it as well as I do."

"Get out of my home, Brian. Now. I have nothing more to say to you."

He grabbed her hands and jerked her forward to stand between his thighs. "Don't run away, Carrie, not again. This isn't the past. It's the here and now, and the future. No one wants to manipulate you, least of all me, but I can't let you throw away the best thing that's happened to either one of us in years."

"I'll decide for myself what's best for me. No one else has the right, not even you."

He plowed ahead, unable to stop himself even though he could see that she was shutting down emotionally. "Fear cripples, then it turns a person into a coward. You're so afraid to take any risks that you're doing to yourself now what your parents did to you after the assault. Think about it, why don't you? For God's sake, really think about it, because you're about to turn yourself into what you claim you don't want to be. A coward and a cripple."

Stricken, she stared at him. She suddenly

wrenched her hands from his grasp, then grabbed the counter edge for balance. Her gaze remained riveted on his face.

Brian swore when he saw the devastation he'd caused, then stormed out of the house.

ELEVEN

Carrie spent the next four days wrestling with her emotions, her conscience, and the truths couched in Brian's angry words. Because she felt reluctant to burden anyone with the dilemma she faced, she took a leave of absence from the Crisis Center.

She walked countless miles on the beach, slept when her memories of the exquisite pleasure she'd found in Brian's passionate embrace eased long enough to allow her a respite, and reflected on the manner in which her past had affected the life she'd created for herself following the assault.

Her intrinsic honesty forced her to acknowledge that she wasn't altogether pleased with the high walls she'd built around her emotions during the last several years. In her quest to safeguard herself, she knew now that the go-it-alone attitude she'd adopted had eliminated the emotional risks of a long-term relationship with a man she trusted.

Sitting on the sidelines had obvious benefits. She hadn't gotten hurt, nor had she been betrayed, but neither had she experienced any real personal happiness.

With no one to turn to, to share either happy or hard times with, and without the fulfillment of her dream of having children, loneliness had been her constant companion. She hated the prospect of that trend continuing, but she feared it would.

Had Brian been right when he'd accused her of cowardice? She'd never thought of herself as a coward; rather, she considered herself a survivor. Now she wasn't so certain exactly what she'd become since the assault.

She felt a combination of surprise, relief, and disappointment as the days passed and Brian's silence persisted. Carrie half expected to find him camped out on her doorstep each morning, his forceful personality provoking additional confrontations. He made no unscheduled appearances, however, and he didn't call.

His absence, all the more glaring when she recalled their time together at the Big Bear Lake cabin, forced her to grapple with the prospect of a life without him. Her mind produced a series of empty colorless years that added to her already melancholy mood.

Could she give him what he deserved from a woman in a committed relationship? Or would she wind up disappointing them both? She also wondered if he'd mistaken feelings of compassion, perhaps even pity for her, for genuine caring.

He'd never used the word *love*, but he'd fought her tooth and nail when she'd asked him to give her time alone. She sensed that he'd risked her complete withdrawal because he felt compelled to fight for her, not just himself.

But why? she asked herself over and over again. Why?

Did he simply care about her as a person, or did he have feelings of love for her? Did he feel compelled to rescue her, or did he actually want to treat her as an equal partner?

No closer to resolving the multitude of unanswered questions by the end of their time apart, Carrie appeared at the judicial complex in San Diego in response to a summons from the district attorney's office. She repeated her account of the robbery, this time in even greater detail because of the stenographer in attendance, and then she answered questions posed by the various attorneys assigned to the prosecution team preparing the case.

Once they thanked her for her cooperation, Carrie made her way out of the conference room. Although relieved that the extensive interview was over for the afternoon, she realized that there would be additional meetings with the staff in the months ahead. She knew from personal experience how tedious and draining the entire legal process could be.

Carrie paused at a water fountain in the hallway for a drink to cool her throat following the lengthy session. As she straightened to resume her walk to the elevator that would take her to the parking garage, she came face-to-face with Brian.

She stumbled to a stop, aware that she shouldn't have been shocked to run into him, since his testimony was also integral to the DA's case. She studied him, her gaze hungrily roaming over his hard-featured face and powerfully constructed body. Her pulse picked up speed, and her pounding heart almost deafened her. She'd missed him, missed him so much that she ached to walk directly into his arms, but she sensed that to indulge herself now with even the slightest physical contact would lead to her downfall.

He looked tense and tired. She knew she looked the same, so she refrained from making any obvious comments.

"Hello," she whispered as she gripped her purse.

"Hello, yourself. I guess I don't need to ask how you're doing?"

She shrugged. "It's been a long four days." And nights, she thought to herself.

"Lousy is a better word."

She sighed, then confessed, "Lonely too."

He nodded. "Very lonely."

She scanned his face, worried about him as she

took in the shadows that smudged the skin beneath his dark eyes and the lines of tension that seemed etched into the skin around his mouth. "You look exhausted," Carrie said, not able to stop herself from voicing her concern.

He shrugged dismissively. "Can't sleep. I've pretty much stopped trying."

"I understand. I'm having the same problem, even though I take a lot of walks and read to try to put myself to sleep at night."

Several people emerged from a nearby office. Taking Carrie's arm, Brian guided her out of the flow of traffic and into a deserted alcove that, by the look of the furnishings, doubled as a mini–conference room.

Carrie stepped to one side of the double-door entry. She didn't feel like having an audience. Butterflies did a frantic midair ballet in her stomach as she watched Brian. "I was called in by the district attorney for the second phase of interviews."

"Me too. I spent several hours with them before lunch."

She frowned, aware that it was almost four in the afternoon. "Why are you still here?"

"I wanted to talk to you. Figured this was as good a place as any."

He'd waited for her, she realized, a little dazed that he'd even made the effort after the way they'd parted. She wasn't sure what to say.

Brian tucked his hands into his trouser pockets, the gesture straining the fabric across his groin and upper thighs.

Carrie's gaze dipped and held. She remembered then, remembered touching him, kissing him, tasting him until she thought she might go mad from the desire that threatened his control and pulsed with life in every cell of her body. She looked away, trying to stop the heat streaming into her veins and the hunger that swept across her senses like a brushfire destined to incinerate everything in its path. She failed.

Brian cleared his throat. "I owe you an apology for coming down on you so hard the other night. You had every right to throw me out."

Shocked, she lifted her gaze to his face. She didn't doubt his sincerity, because she knew that apologies didn't come easily to a man like Brian. "We were both under a lot of pressure, and we both said things we probably didn't even mean."

"I think you were in shock after everything that had happened between us," he said.

"I was," she admitted, not surprised that he'd cut to the bottom line. That was his style. "I probably still am on some levels. It had been so long since . . ." She faltered, suddenly unable to express the liberation of body and spirit that he'd orchestrated.

". . . since anyone had made you feel?"

"Yes," Carrie breathed, caught off-guard by his sensitivity.

How many men would understand what a

shock it was to a woman's mind and body to experience real emotional and physical intimacy for the very first time at the age of thirty-five? She still felt the reverberations deep in her soul when she sat quietly and let herself remember the sensuality of this man and his skill as a lover.

"What are you thinking?" he asked.

She managed a faint smile, but it reflected the weariness of her heart and spirit. "That I'm glad you were the one to take me off the shelf."

He closed the space between them, pausing just inches away from her. "I've missed you."

Trembling from the simultaneous impact of the heat emanating from his body and the faint citrusy scent of his cologne, she struggled with her emotions. "I miss you, too, but . . ."

"Say it," he urged as he reached for her hand.

". . . I'm still trying to make some sense out of this situation."

"This may be the only thing that will ever make sense between us," he muttered.

Brian leaned down then, blocking out the light from the wall of windows nearby. He took her mouth, his lips playing over hers, first with great tenderness, then with increased hunger.

Carrie gasped and arched against him, her senses coming alive like an electric current that had been switched to full power.

He darted his tongue into her mouth, groaning as hers stabbed and dueled in response.

Her purse slid out of her fingers and dropped

to the floor. She didn't care. She cared only about Brian and feeling alive again. Slipping her arms around his waist, she angled her head, encouraging even greater intimacy.

He supplied it when he plunged his tongue into her mouth and ate at her like a starved man.

She responded instinctively and in kind, her hunger for him just as intense and volatile. Carrie moaned into his mouth, her hands traveling frantically up and down his back as she submerged herself in the flavors and textures of his passion. Brian tasted of seduction and sensuality, of light and darkness, of things forbidden but utterly necessary to her survival.

As he drank from her lips and caressed her body, Carrie felt overwhelmed, consumed, and then reborn. She fought the doubts filtering into her mind and shaking her confidence. She resisted relinquishing the sense of rightness that touching him and being touched by him provided.

But reality crashed headlong into the fantasy, shattering the perfection of the moment. She died a little inside, then went absolutely still in his arms.

"What?" he asked, his voice rough and low, his breath hot as it washed across the side of her neck.

Carrie rested her forehead against his chin, her breathing ragged, her entire body shaking.

Bracketing her hips between his hands, Brian

shifted her forward and moved against her. He groaned, the sound going on forever.

She felt his heat and hardness, not simply the shudder that ripped through him. Her knees threatened to give way. She struggled to catch her breath.

"Please listen to me, Brian. Please," she whispered, feeling the strength of his desire, wanting that strength deep inside of her more than anything, but still keenly aware that she couldn't always have what she wanted.

He lifted his head and dragged air into his body, then exhaled. "I'm listening."

"Nothing's changed since we were together," she insisted. "I'm still not ready to talk to you."

His jaw tightened. "You're serious, aren't you?"

"Yes." She couldn't stand the disappointment in his expression, so she glanced away.

He forced her to look at him when he cupped her chin and brought her face back into view.

She closed her eyes.

"Look at me, Carrie."

She did, but very reluctantly. She felt ashamed and too immature for words, and she knew she couldn't go on this way much longer. It would destroy them both.

"You're running out of time."

Anger sparked to life inside her. Her defenses lined up like an army around her heart. "Are you giving me a deadline?"

"Of course not, but I think you're overanalyzing. Why don't you just let yourself feel?"

She moved backward, grateful when he didn't try to stop her. "Because I'm thirty-five years old, and I realize that life is more complicated than feelings. Reality counts, Brian, especially since we both have to deal with it."

"You're determined to run from anyone or anything that doesn't fit neatly into your life, aren't you?"

"I'm not running. I'm facing facts."

"You're using facts from the past as a reason not to have a future. Why, Carrie? Just tell me why?"

"I don't want your pity!" She heard the words leave her mouth, and she couldn't believe that she'd abandoned her pride and confessed her greatest fear.

"That's the craziest damn thing I've ever heard."

"Is it? I don't think so." She leaned down and rescued her purse from the floor. "*You* are the one who's making me crazy right now."

An incredulous expression on his face, Brian refuted her earlier remark. "I don't pity you. I'm in love with you, dammit!"

Stunned, she opened her mouth to speak, then snapped it closed a second later.

"I love you," he said, his voice lower this time. He extended his hand to her. "Haven't you figured that out yet?"

She didn't reach back. She shook her head instead, wanting to believe him, but knowing she couldn't risk it. Intent on escape, Carrie edged toward the double doors that led out to the hallway.

"You're running again!"

She didn't bother to deny the truth of his accusation. "I need to think."

"Then think. I'm not trying to stop you, but think clearly before you wreck both our lives."

"I can't. Not here."

"Stop running, Carrie!"

She darted out of the room and into the crowded hallway. Instead of waiting to board an elevator, she raced down the stairs to the parking garage.

Brian's words echoed in her head like a chant as she drove out of the city and up the coast to her home.

Stop running!

Stop running!

Brian found Carrie on the patio behind her house an hour later. Clad in a turquoise silk caftan, she sat huddled on the chaise longue, her arms circling her updrawn legs and her chin parked on her knees.

"You left your front door unlocked," he said in the quiet tone reserved for skittish animals and small children as he approached her. "You need to be more careful, Carrie."

She absently nodded, but she didn't look up as he sat down on the lower half of the chaise.

As he studied her pale features in the diminishing summer evening light, Brian couldn't help thinking about the battle she'd single-handedly fought when her innocence had been taken from her, the strength of character required of her to survive an act of violence that would have destroyed a lesser woman, and her ability to turn a tragedy into a personal commitment to the recovery of those who faced a similar crisis.

How could he not love this woman? he wondered, his gaze traveling over her.

Carrie possessed every trait he'd ever valued and then some, although her stubbornness wore on his nerves at times. He loved her with a depth of feeling that startled him. He loved her unconditionally, and he couldn't recall ever feeling that way about a woman before. He loved what he saw as her uniqueness as a person, and he loved her passion. He loved the idea of sharing a home with her, then filling it with children they would cherish together. He'd waited his entire forty years for a chance at this kind of happiness, a sense of belonging to something greater than himself, and he couldn't let go now.

Brian suspected that Carrie loved him, if only a little. His suspicion, based as much on hope as on her behavior in recent days, fueled his determination to break through the wall of silence she persisted in using as a shield to protect her fragile emotions.

He knew that his future—their future—might hinge on what he said next, so he chose his words with care. A relentless fighter all of his life, Brian didn't intend to lose the proverbial war, although he knew he'd lost a few of their recent battles.

"I cannot and will not give up on you, Carrie Forbes, so don't expect that of me. Not ever. I love you, and I want to marry you," he said, his tone subdued but firm.

She gave him a stunned look. "But why?"

"Why not?"

She flinched. "To rescue me? I told you, I don't want your pity, Brian. That's the last thing I could handle from you."

"What I feel for you isn't even remotely connected to pity. You're the last person in the world I'd ever pity, although I hate the pain you've endured. Had it been in my power, I would have saved you the ordeal you experienced. As for rescuing you, you've already accomplished that task yourself. I'm not some knight in shining armor, Carrie. I'm just a very flawed man who met a woman during a bank robbery and then fell in love with her."

She finally made eye contact with him, this time her gaze steady as she peered at him.

What he saw in her expression gave him the

first bit of hope he'd had in several days. "I said I love you, and I mean it."

"I'm afraid to . . ." She paused uncertainly.

Brian supplied some of the thoughts he'd had in recent days as he'd tried to understand what was really troubling her. He prayed it would help her. "I don't think you're really afraid, but I do think you're worried about several valid issues, because some bastard almost succeeded in destroying your life fourteen years ago. Because someone you trusted madc you feel helpless when he victimized you. Because you've struggled to take control of your life and now you're worried that you'll have to give up that control if you let down your guard. Because you care enough about me to try to protect my happiness, despite the misguided way you're going about it."

She inhaled shakily, nodded, then exhaled in a rush. "There's more."

"Tell me," he encouraged as he took her hands, the love he felt for her and the compassion that was deeply ingrained in his own character reflected in his dark eyes and intense expression.

Carrie gripped his hands. "I'm afraid I'll become a burden to you because of my past. I'm also afraid that I'll fail to live up to your expectations. I don't want to disappoint you."

"That won't happen," he said with absolute conviction.

"You sound so sure."

"I am."

"Why? How?" she questioned.

He took a calculated risk and voiced his suspicion, his hope. "Because you love me."

Carrie nodded. "I do love you. I love you more deeply than I ever thought I could love a man, which is why I don't want to risk causing you unhappiness. *I'm* the one who's no prize, Brian."

"You can't make my decisions for me. The risk is mine to take. I obviously have more faith in you than you currently have in yourself." He paused for a moment, then said, "I think we need to work on that, because it's a definite problem. Do you still trust me?"

"I've always trusted you."

Standing, Brian drew her up from the chaise and lifted her into his arms. He carried her across the patio, through the kitchen, and down the hallway to her bedroom.

He undressed her in the dusky shadows as they stood beside her bed. Any resistance on her part would have stopped him, but Brian sensed that she understood his motivation, sensed as well that she needed him as much as he needed her.

Carrie didn't utter a single syllable. Not one. She just watched his face, the light that had been missing from her hazel eyes slowly returning as he disrobed.

As he smoothed his fingertips up her slender arms, across her shoulders, and then down over the tips of her breasts, he felt some of the rigidity leave her body. The tension that replaced it had nothing to do with stress and everything to do with desire, he knew.

"Love me enough to trust our feelings for each other. Love me enough to build a future with me, Carrie Forbes, because I don't want to think about what my life will be like if you aren't a part of it."

Carrie arched into his hands when he cupped her breasts in his palms, then trembled as he flicked his thumbs across her nipples. They puckered into tight buds, tingling with sensations that streamed like rivers of flame into the lower regions of her body.

Sucking in a deep breath, she raised a shaking hand to his face and cupped his cheek. "I almost believe it's possible, Brian."

"You will," he promised. He nudged her backward until her legs bumped against the bed. "Let yourself love me. You won't regret it."

She looped her arms around his neck and went up on tiptoes, her breasts flattening against his chest and her hips fitting perfectly to his loins. "I want you so much," she whispered.

He smiled. Some of his worry departed, but not all of it. He knew that they still had more talking to do, but he believed that Carrie needed to be reminded of her own innate sensuality before they continued the conversation they'd begun on the patio.

Determined to help her find the peace of mind she needed in order to embrace the idea of a future together, Brian felt no guilt in using seduction as a tactic to persuade her to see all the possibilities of a shared life. Easing her down onto the mattress, he drew her into his arms and claimed her mouth in a hard, scintillating kiss that left her trembling and gasping for breath several minutes later.

Brian encouraged Carrie to become the aggressor in the minutes that followed, although she didn't realize it. He repeatedly pushed her to the edge of her tolerance, then insisted that she express her desires. She did with breathlessly inarticulate little cries that enflamed his senses and his hunger for her.

He teased her unmercifully, using his hands and mouth on her until she experienced a series of orgasms that shook her to her core. He refused to give her a moment of relief, his intentions becoming clear as he tantalized and teased, bringing her to the edge of madness, cooling her down, and then starting the process all over again.

He provoked and tormented her, then sent her spinning beyond control over and over again, until he felt as if he were embracing a wild creature of nature. He stayed with her every step of the way.

Carrie turned on him in sensual frustration, any inhibitions she might have felt vanishing, her instincts clearly her guide. She repaid Brian for each and every foray he'd conducted. Her fingertips traveled over his body, deliberately provocative, inciting with every stroke. Her lips were feverish as she explored every inch of his naked body.

She aroused with a total absence of mercy, especially when she knelt between his parted thighs, her hands roving up and down his muscular legs before she combed her fingers through the coarse nest of hair that framed his maleness.

She tortured him when she leaned down and blew hot gusts of air across his straining flesh, then with delicate swipes of her tongue. She took him into her mouth, loving him so thoroughly that he shuddered and fisted his hands in the sheets beneath his writhing body.

Laughing softly, Carrie increased his sensual torment when she mounted him without warning. She sank down slowly until he was embedded so deeply inside her that the separateness of their two bodies ceased and no longer mattered. Raising herself up without breaking contact, she leaned forward, seeking balance and leverage as she braced herself with her hands on his chest.

When she began making circular motions with her hips, Brian sucked in a harsh breath, grabbed her, and tried to hold her still. He felt close to exploding.

"No fair," she insisted before dropping a light kiss on his lips. "This is my game, so the rules are mine to make."

He gentled his hold on her. "You'll pay for this," he vowed.

She nibbled on his lower lip, then laved the area with the tip of her tongue. "I already have," she reminded him as she lowered her hips once again and deepened his penetration.

He felt as though he'd been sucked into a narrow channel of liquid fire. She dipped and swayed atop him, then moved in that same circular pattern that had almost completely ravaged his control a few minutes earlier.

"You're killing me," he groaned a short while later.

"But very sweetly," she asserted. Her eyes fell closed, and her head tipped to one side as she rode him.

The dreamy expression on her face entranced him, and the undulating glide of her hair across her shoulders made him think of a silky auburn waterfall. Brian framed her face with his hands. "You are exquisite."

She opened her eyes and smiled at him. Her body intimately linked with his, she began to flow sideways, encouraging him to follow her with soft murmurs of encouragement.

Momentarily concerned, Brian held her still before rolling atop her. He wanted to be sure that she understood what she was inviting.

"It's all right," she said. "I want you above me."

His love for her expanded in that breathless moment, as did the pride he felt in her. He understood her meaning. She trusted him, really trusted him now. Brian tucked her beneath him, certain that her confidence in herself and in him had eliminated her fear of being physically dominated or overpowered.

"Don't hold back," she whispered against his lips before blistering his senses with a hot, open-mouthed kiss that devastated even as it inspired.

Brian discovered that he couldn't hold back any longer, so he didn't bother trying. He surged deeply into her, savoring the tight wet heat of her, savoring as well the unrestrained quality of her response to him.

Thrusting repeatedly into the depths of her writhing body, he felt the change in Carrie the instant her body surrendered to the inevitable. He felt, too, the love he craved from her, the sense of finally finding an emotional home that would always welcome him.

A storm seized them both, a storm of rich sensuality, emotional fulfillment, and physical harmony that took total control of their merged bodies.

Carrie cried out, stiffened suddenly, and then came apart beneath him. She unraveled completely, clinging to Brian and repeatedly gasping his name as her entire body quaked.

He felt both the quivering shocks that rippled through her and the tumult of his own impending release. He pounded into her, possessively and as deeply as nature allowed, compelled to imprint himself on her heart and soul and body for all eternity.

As Carrie went reeling into a world of pure sensation, a world where nothing mattered but the two people sharing a quest for mutual fulfillment, Brian followed her. He surrendered to the remarkable woman in his arms and to the pleasure-filled oblivion of release. He groaned, his final thought that together they'd surpassed every secret fantasy he'd ever had about loving and being loved.

TWELVE

Brian reached for Carrie in his sleep, but his search yielded little more than empty air and rumpled sheets. He wakened abruptly, realizing that he was alone.

Sitting up in bed, he looked around the room, the light from the moon that cascaded through nearby windows providing limited visibility. He glanced at the luminous dial of the clock on the nightstand, discovering that it was well after midnight.

Shoving aside the covers, he got out of bed and stepped into his trousers. Brian consciously quelled the uneasiness that Carrie's absence caused, telling himself that their hours of lovemaking had dispelled many of her doubts. He didn't want to consider any other reason for her departure from bed in the middle of the night, even though he knew he should.

He made his way down the hallway to the living room, which looked out onto the backyard. Relief spiraled through him when he spotted her.

Carrie stood naked in a shaft of moonlight, her attention captured by the view from a wall of undraped windows of the star-studded night sky. The hourglass perfection of her body eclipsed nature's display and made him pause in the doorway for a moment.

He thought then about what she would look like swollen with his child. The image his mind produced caused his breath to catch, sent a rush of heat into his bloodstream, and stirred his desire for her yet again. His body responded, forcing him to tamp down the arousal that resulted.

Once he regained control, Brian exhaled, the sound audible in the silence of the still house.

Carrie didn't move, but she asked, "Did I wake you when I got out of bed a little while ago?"

"No. I just missed you, that's all."

"How could you miss me? You were sleeping so soundly, and we . . ."

". . . and we made love for hours on end?" he finished for her.

"Yes."

"You've obviously put a curse on me."

She laughed at his absurd remark as she turned to look at him. "I've been thinking."

"That doesn't surprise me." He crossed the

room to stand beside her, his gaze fixed on the woman who'd captured his heart. "Beautiful."

"Isn't it?" she whispered, her eyes scanning the night sky. "I'm glad we made love."

Some of his worry departed. He smiled at her as he slipped his arm around her shoulders and drew her against him. "Hopefully, we'll do it again soon."

She sobered, then gazed up at him.

"Talk to me," he invited.

"Bill . . . the man I almost married . . . used to call me the Ice Queen."

"He was a fool," Brian said. "He's not worth thinking about."

"I know you're right, but his words hurt all the same. I stopped letting myself feel after I ended the engagement. I actually stopped wanting to feel, because I was tired of the heartache it caused. That's why I've been so locked up inside for so long."

"As far as I'm concerned, you could melt the polar ice cap in under five seconds."

She laughed softly. "I don't recognize myself when we're together. I feel so much, and sometimes it overwhelms me. I worry some of the time that I might not always be this way with you."

"You're chasing old ghosts. I'll make you a gift of my confidence in us."

"Life isn't usually that simple," she remarked.

"It can be, if you'll let it. It's a matter of choice, Carrie. Your choice."

"I want to make the right one, for both our sakes."

"I think you already have, especially since you're not afraid of me."

"I never have been. Please believe me when I tell you that fear is not an issue when we make love, Brian, because it's the truth."

"Then we have a place to start, don't we?" he asked.

He drew her to a position in front of him so that they could both watch the stars glittering like tiny diamond chips in the midnight sky. He cupped her breasts, savoring the softness of her skin and the way in which her nipples beaded under his stroking fingertips.

As he caressed her Carrie moaned softly. Tingling sensations sparkled throughout her body. She responded quickly, intensely, despite the indulgent hours of lovemaking they'd already shared.

She trembled, her head falling back against his chest when one of his hands drifted down her midriff and over the gentle swell of her stomach. His fingers moved through the silk at the top of her thighs. She parted her legs, the spontaneous gesture an invitation that he accepted when he dipped two narrow fingers into the damp heat of her body.

Tiny interior muscles clutched at his fingers. He lowered his head, his lips skimming up and down the side of her neck as he explored her body.

She whispered his name, the shattered sound more arousing than he would have ever believed possible. He shifted against her, his maleness pressing against her buttocks despite the fabric of his trousers.

"I can barely stand up right now," she confessed.

He chuckled. "And I can't seem to stop touching you."

"I'd hate it if you did."

Because of Brian, she felt desire. Because of Brian, she'd found both physical and emotional fulfillment. Because of Brian, she possessed hope for the future. Because of Brian, she believed that happiness was within her reach.

He withdrew his hand, smoothing it over her stomach before looping his arms around her and hugging her to him. "Tell me what else you've been thinking about."

"I want you again," nearly spilled past her lips, but she mastered her hunger for him. She gathered her wits, breathing deeply for several quiet moments, and then admitted, "I was thinking about some of the things you said yesterday afternoon when we were downtown."

"I can't apologize this time, Carrie."

She turned in his loose embrace to look up at him. "I don't expect you to. You were being honest with me about how you felt."

"I hurt you."

She shook her head. "No, you didn't. You shocked me, and I should thank you. You made me really think about us. I don't want to run anymore, Brian. I'm sick of running, of feeling incomplete, of being afraid to love. It stops now."

He tightened his embrace. "We make a good team, in spite of the past. I'm referring to my past, not just yours, you know."

She settled back against him. "Your body reminds me of a heater. I love it."

Brian laughed at her verbal left turn. "Thanks, I think."

"Talk," she commanded gently.

They both knew why and about what.

Brian spoke honestly. "You were right about anyone over the age of fifteen having baggage from the past, even though I resisted the idea at first. I felt like a real failure after the divorce. I knew I was guilty of neglect. I used to tell myself that I was building something important for both of us, but I was lying to salve my conscience. I made a conscious choice to put all my energy into my work. In my gut, I knew I was jeopardizing my relationship with Gloria."

"Hasn't it occurred to you that by accepting your behavior, she approved of it?" Carrie asked.

"It occurred to me, but I figured I was rationalizing the situation, trying to excuse myself."

"I think you're being too hard on yourself."

He arched an eyebrow. "Something else we have in common, I guess."

"You're probably right," Carrie agreed.

He smoothed his broad-palmed hands across her slender shoulders. "You aren't the only one who'd stopped feeling, and you aren't the only one who lost hope."

Tears welled in her eyes. She realized not for the first time that Brian, despite his obvious strengths and successes, was still vulnerable. She knew now the courage it had taken for him to keep fighting for her, and she also knew that to abandon their love would be the most cowardly of actions on her part.

She loved him, and she couldn't imagine her life without him. She didn't even want to imagine it.

"You're very quiet," he said.

She blinked, refocusing on Brian's face. It was then that she saw his tension. Reaching up, she gently caressed his cheek. "I'm fine."

He studied her for a moment, then nodded. Drawing her into his arms, he fitted her against his hard body, a shudder moving through him as she twined her arms around his neck. "It's our destiny to be together, Carrie Forbes. Will you trust me enough to marry me?"

"Of course I'll marry you."

"Of course?"

"I'm not nearly as foolish as you might think."

He searched her features. "I don't think you're

foolish, just so damn stubborn some of the time that I want to take you and shake you."

"How about making love to me instead, when I get out of line?" she suggested playfully.

He lifted her up, cradling her against his chest, and carried her back to her bedroom.

"Am I out of line already?"

"I thought I'd eliminate the possibility in advance," he informed her as he dumped her into the center of the bed and started to remove his trousers.

Carrie watched him, openly admiring his muscular anatomy.

"See something you like?" Brian asked as he joined her on the bed.

"I like it all. I want it all."

"Greedy. I like that in a woman."

She laughed as he tumbled her onto her back, then came down over her. "Someone very wise once told me that it takes two people to make a marriage work and two people to cause a marriage to fail. That wise woman has been happily married for more than forty years."

Brian smiled. "Sounds like she knows what she's doing."

Carrie grinned, thinking of Elizabeth. "She keeps her husband guessing all the time. She's really quite amazing."

"Will you keep me guessing?" he asked as he nibbled on her chin.

"Only some of the time. Most of the time,"

she whispered against his lips before he claimed them, "I'll just love you."

They made love then with the kind of tenderness that only commitment can foster. Later, when they'd temporarily exhausted their bodies, they returned to the patio, stretched out together on the chaise longue, and watched the dawn spill across the early-morning sky.

"I want babies," Carrie said.

"As many as you'd like."

"Let's start with one."

"Now?" he asked, pulling her atop him before he started to separate the lapels of her robe.

She shook her head. "This afternoon. You've worn me out, and I need to rest."

Brian hugged her to him, then nipped at the fragrant skin of her neck.

"I like this neighborhood," she said after a while.

"My place is larger."

"Then we'll live there."

"You're very cooperative."

"I'm very well loved. It makes me easy."

He laughed.

She loved the sound. "I forgot to ask. Can you afford a wife and children?"

"I have a few million set aside for a rainy day. We'll manage, although I may have to put you on a budget."

"In that case, I'll use my own money."

"Does this mean I'm marrying a rich woman?"

"Comfortable." She wiggled her hips, settling more firmly between his thighs. "Very comfortable."

"Good, you can support me in my old age."

"You've got a deal, but only after we've gotten all the children through college."

Brian nodded, his hands framing her face, his expression intent as he studied her. "You really do love me, don't you?"

Carrie heard his disbelief. "More than you'll ever know."

"I'll always want to know. Always," he pledged.

THE EDITORS' CORNER

Along with May flowers come four fabulous LOVESWEPTs that will dazzle you with humor, excitement, and, above all, love. Touching, tender, packed with emotion and wonderfully happy endings, our four upcoming romances are real treasures.

Starting the lineup is the innovative Ruth Owen with **AND BABIES MAKE FOUR**, LOVESWEPT #786. Naked to the waist, his jeans molded to his thighs like a second skin, Sam Donovan looks like trouble—untamed and shameless! Dr. Noel Revere hadn't expected her guide to the island's sacred places to be so uncivilized, but this rebel sets her blood on fire and stirs her insides like a runaway hurricane. Can they survive a journey into the jungle shared by two matchmaking computers with mating on their minds? Once again,

Ruth Owen delivers an exotic adventure that is both wildly sexy and wickedly funny!

In her enchanting debut novel, **KISS AND TELL**, LOVESWEPT #787, Suzanne Brockmann adds a dash of mystery to a favorite romantic fantasy. When Dr. Marshall Devlin spots Leila Hunt alone on the dance floor, he yearns to charm the violet-eyed Cinderella into his arms, but how can he court the lady when they fight over everything, and always have? Then the clock strikes twelve and Leila is possessed by the passion of a familiar stranger. He captures her lips—and her soul—in a moment of magic, but can she learn to love the man behind the mask?

From award-winning author Terry Lawrence comes **FUGITIVE FATHER**, LOVESWEPT #788. A single light burned in the window of the isolated lakeside cottage, but Ben Renfield wondered which was the greater risk—hiding in the woods to evade his pursuers or seeking refuge with a beautiful stranger! Touched by his need, tempted by her own, Bridget Bernard trades precious solitude for perilous intimacy . . . and feels her own walls begin to crack. Can rescuing a lonely warrior transform her own destiny? Terry Lawrence blends simmering suspense and stunning sensuality in a tale that explores the tender mysteries of the human heart.

Finally, there's **STILL MR. & MRS.**, LOVESWEPT #789, by talented newcomer Patricia Olney. Two years before, they'd embraced in a heated moment, courted in one sultry afternoon, and wed in a reckless promise to cherish forever. Now Gabriel and Rebecca Stewart are days from the heart-breaking end of a dream! When a business crisis demands a last-minute lover's charade, Gabe offers Reb anything she wants—but will their seductive game of "let's pretend" ignite flames of dangerous desire? In this delicious story of second chances, Patricia Olney makes us believe in the enduring miracle of love.

Happy reading!

With warmest wishes,

Beth de Guzman

Shauna Summers

Beth de Guzman	Shauna Summers
Senior Editor	Editor

P.S. Watch for these Bantam women's fiction titles coming in April: From the *New York Times* bestselling author Betina Krahn comes another blockbuster romance filled with her patented brand of love and laughter in **THE UNLIKELY ANGEL.** Also welcome nationally bestselling author Iris Johansen in her hardcover debut of **THE UGLY DUCKLING,** a tale of contemporary romantic suspense! **DANGEROUS TO HOLD** by Elizabeth Thornton is filled with her trademark passion and suspense, and **THE REBEL AND THE REDCOAT** by Karyn

Monk promises a scorching tale of passion set against the dramatic backdrop of the American Revolution! Be sure to see next month's LOVESWEPTs for a preview of these exceptional novels. And immediately following this page, preview the Bantam women's fiction titles on sale now!

A tantalizing tale of a legendary knight and a headstrong lady whose daring quest for a mysterious crystal will draw them into a whirlwind of treachery—and desire.

From *New York Times* bestseller

Amanda Quick

comes

MYSTIQUE

When the fearsome knight called Hugh the Relentless swept into Lingwood Manor like a storm, everyone cowered—except Lady Alice. Sharp-tongued and unrepentant, the flame-haired beauty believed Sir Hugh was not someone to dread but the fulfillment of her dreams. She knew he had come for the dazzling green crystal, knew he would be displeased to find that it was no longer in her possession. Yet Alice had a proposition for the dark and forbidding knight: In return for a dowry that would free Alice and her brother from their uncle's grasp, she would lend her powers of detection to his warrior's skills and together they would recover his treasured stone. But even as Hugh accepted her terms, he added a condition of his own: Lady Alice must agree to a temporary betrothal—one that would soon draw her deep into Hugh's great stone fortress, and into a battle that could threaten their lives . . . and their only chance at love.

From the winner of the Romantic Times *Storyteller of the Year Award comes*

DIABLO

by **Patricia Potter**

Raised in a notorious outlaw hideout, Nicky Thompson learned to shoot fast, ride hard, and hold her own against killers and thieves. Yet nothing in her experience prepared her for the new brand of danger that just rode in. Ruggedly handsome, with an easy strength and a hint of deviltry in his smile, Diablo made Nicky's heart race not with fright but with a sizzling arousal. When she challenged him to taste her womanly charms, she didn't know he was a condemned convict who'd come to Sanctuary with one secret purpose—to destroy it in exchange for pardons for himself and a friend. Would a renegade hungry for freedom jeopardize his dangerous mission for a last chance at love?

With a sigh of pure contentment, Kane relaxed in the big tin bathtub in an alcove off the barber's shop. One hand rubbed his newly shaved cheek. The barber had been good, the water hot. The shave had been sheer luxury, costing five times what it would have in any other town, but that didn't bother him. In truth, it amused him. He was spending Marshal Ben Masters's money.

He lit a long, thin cigar that he'd purchased, also at a rather high price. He supposed he was as close to heaven as he was apt to get. Sinking deeper into the water, he tried not to think beyond this immediate pleasure. But he couldn't forget his friend Davy. The leash, as Masters so coldly called it, pulled tight around his neck.

Reluctantly, he rose from the tub and pulled on the new clothes he'd purchased at the general store. Blue denim trousers, a dark blue shirt. A clean bandanna around his neck. The old one had been beyond redemption. He ran a comb through his freshly washed hair, trying to tame it, and regarded himself briefly in the mirror. The scar stood out. It was one of the few he'd earned honorably, but it was like a brand, forever identifying him as Diablo.

Hell, what difference did it make? He wasn't here to court. He was here to betray. He couldn't forget that. Not for a single moment.

With a snort of self-disgust, he left the room for the stable. He would explore the boundaries of Sanctuary, do a reconnaissance. He had experience at that. Lots of experience.

Nicky rode for an hour before she heard gunshots.

She headed toward the sound, knowing full well that a stray bullet could do as much damage as a directed one. Her brother Robin was crouching, a gunbelt wrapped around his lean waist, his hand on the grip of a six-shooter. In a quick movement, he pulled it from the holster and aimed at a target affixed to a tree. Then he saw Nicky.

The pride on his face faltered, and then he set his jaw rebelliously and fired. He missed.

Nicky turned her attention to the man next to him. Arrogance radiated from him as he leered at her. Her skin crawling, she rode over to them and addressed Cobb Yancy. "If my uncle knew about this, you would be out of Sanctuary faster than a bullet from that gun."

"That so, honey?" Yancy drawled. "Then he'd have to do something about your baby brother, wouldn't he?" He took the gun from Robin and stood there, letting it dangle from his fingers.

Nicky held out her hand. "Give me the gun."

"Why don't you take it from me?" Yancy's voice was low, inviting.

"You leave now, and I'll forget about this," she said.

"What if I don't want you to forget about it?" he asked, moving toward her horse. "The boy can take your horse back. You can ride with me." His hand was suddenly on the horse's halter.

"Robin can walk back," she said, trying to back Molly. Yancy's grasp, though, was too strong.

Yancy turned to Robin. "You do that, boy. Start walking."

Robin looked from Yancy to Nicky and back again, apprehension beginning to show in his face. "I'd rather ride back with you, Mr. Yancy."

The gun was suddenly pointed at Robin. "Do as I say. Your sister and I will be along later."

Nicky was stiff with anger and not a little fear. "My uncle will kill you," Nicky pointed out.

"He may try," Yancy said. "I've been wondering if he's as fast as everyone says."

Nicky knew then that Cobb Yancy had just been looking for an excuse to try her uncle. Had he scented weakness? Was he after Sanctuary?

She felt for the small derringer she'd tucked inside a pocket in her trousers. "Go on, Robin," she said. "I'll catch up to you."

Robin didn't move.

"Go," she ordered in a voice that had gone hard.

Softness didn't survive here, not in these mountains, not among these men.

Instead of obeying her, Robin lunged for the gun in Yancy's hand. It went off, and Robin went down. Nicky aimed her derringer directly at Yancy's heart and fired.

He looked stunned as the gun slipped from his fingers and he went down on his knees, then toppled over. Nicky dismounted and ran over to Robin. Blood was seeping from a wound in his shoulder.

She heard hoofbeats and grabbed the gun Yancy had been holding. It could be his brother coming.

But it wasn't. It was Diablo, looking very different than he had earlier. He reined in his horse at the sight of the gun aimed in his direction. His gaze moved from her to Robin to the body on the ground.

"Trouble?"

"Nothing I can't handle," Nicky said, keeping the gun pointed at him.

The side of his mouth turned up by the scar inched higher. "I see you can," he said, then studied Robin. "What about him?"

"My brother," she explained stiffly. "That polecat shot him."

"I think he needs some help."

"Not from you, mister," she said.

His brows knitted together, and he shifted in the saddle. Then ignoring the threat in her hand, he slid down from his horse and walked over to Robin, pulling the boy's shirt back to look at the wound.

Robin grimaced, then fixed his concentration on Diablo's scar. "You're that new one," he said. "Diablo."

Diablo nodded. "Some call me that. How in the hell did everyone around know I was coming?"

"There's not many secrets here," Robin said, but his voice was strained. He was obviously trying to be brave for the gunslinger. Nicky sighed. Hadn't he learned anything today?

Diablo studied the wound a moment, then took off his bandanna and gave it to Robin. "It's clean. Hold it to the wound to stop the bleeding."

He then went over to Cobb Yancy, checked for signs of life and found none. He treated death very casually, Nicky noticed. "He's dead, all right," Diablo said.

Before she could protest, he returned to Robin. He helped Robin shed his shirt, which he tore in two and made into a sling. When he was through, he offered a steadying arm to Robin.

"Don't," Nicky said sharply. "I'll help him."

"He's losing blood," Diablo said. "He could lose consciousness. You prepared to take his whole weight?"

Nicky studied her brother's face. It was pale, growing paler by the moment. "We'll send someone back for Yancy. He has a brother. It would be best not to meet him."

Diablo didn't ask any questions, she'd give him that. She looked down at her hands and noticed they were shaking. She'd never killed a man before.

Diablo's eyes seemed to stab through her, reading her thoughts. Then he was guiding Robin to Yancy's horse, practically lifting her brother onto the gelding. There was an easy strength about him, a confidence, that surprised Nicky. He'd looked so much the renegade loner that morning, yet here he'd taken charge automatically, as if he were used to leadership. Resentment mixed with gratitude.

She tucked the gun into the waist of her trousers

and mounted her mare. She kept seeing Yancy's surprised face as he went down. Her hands were shaking even more now. She'd killed a man. A man who had a very dangerous brother.

She had known this would happen one day. But nothing could have prepared her for the despair she felt at taking someone's life. She felt sick inside.

Diablo, who was riding ahead with Robin, looked back. He reined in his own horse until she was abreast of him, and she felt his watchful gaze settle on her. "Tell Yancy's brother I did it."

Nothing he could have said would have surprised her more.

"Why?"

"I can take care of myself."

He couldn't have insulted her more. "And what do you think *I* just did?"

"I think you just killed your first man, and you don't need another on your conscience. You certainly don't need it on your stomach. You look like you're going to upchuck."

She glared at him. "I'm fine."

"Good. Your brother isn't."

All of Nicky's attention went to Robin. He was swaying in his saddle. She moved her horse around to his side. "Just a few more minutes, Robin. Hold on."

"I'm sorry, Sis. I shouldn't have gone with . . . Cobb Yancy, but—"

"Hush," she said. "If you hadn't, Yancy would have found something else. He was after more than me."

But Robin wasn't listening. He was holding on to the saddle horn for dear life, and his face was a white mask now.

"Maybe I should ride ahead," she said. "Get some help."

"You got a doctor in this place?" Diablo asked.

"Not right now. But Andy—"

"Andy?"

"The blacksmith. He knows some medicine, and I can sew up a wound."

"Go on ahead and get him ready," Diablo ordered. "I'll get your brother there." He stopped his horse, slipped off, and then mounted behind Robin, holding him upright in the saddle.

Could she really trust Diablo that much? Dare she leave him alone with Robin?

"I'll take care of him," Diablo said, more gently this time.

Nicky finally nodded and spurred her mare into a gallop.

Wearing it was just asking for trouble

THE BAD LUCK WEDDING DRESS

The most memorable Texas romance yet
from the uniquely talented

Geralyn Dawson

"One of the best new authors to come along in years—fresh, charming, and romantic!"
—*New York Times* bestselling author Jill Barnett

They were calling it the Bad Luck Wedding Dress, and Jenny Fortune knew that spelled trouble for her Fort Worth dressmaking shop. Just because the Bailey girls had met with one mishap or another after wearing Jenny's loveliest creation, her clientele had begun to stay away in droves. Yet Jenny was still betting she could turn her luck around—by wearing the gown herself at her very own wedding. There's just one hitch: first she has to find a groom. . . .

While people all over the world have strange ideas about luck, Fort Worth, being a gambling town, seemed to have stranger ideas than most. Folks here made bets on everything, from the weather to the length of the sermon at the Baptist church on Sunday. Jenny theorized that this practice contributed to a dedicated belief in the vagaries of luck, making it easy for many to lay the blame for the Baileys' difficulties on the dress.

Monique shrugged. "Well, I think you're wrong. Give it a try, dear. It's a perfect solution. And you needn't be overly concerned with your lack of a beau. Despite your father's influence, you are still my daughter. The slightest of efforts will offer you plenty of men from whom to choose. Now, I think you should start with this."

She pulled the pins from Jenny's chignon, fluffed out her wavy blond tresses, then pressed a kiss to her cheek. "I'm so glad I was able to help, dear. Now I'd best get back to the station. Keep me informed about the developments, and if you choose to follow my advice, be sure to telegraph me with the date of the wedding. I'll do my best to see that your father drags his nose from his studies long enough to attend."

"Wait, Monique," Jenny began. But the dressing-room curtains flapped in her mother's wake, and the front door's welcome bell tinkled before she could get out the words "I can't do these back buttons myself."

Wonderful. Simply wonderful. She closed her eyes and sighed. It'd be just her luck if not a single woman entered the shop this afternoon. "The Bad Luck Wedding Dress strikes again," she grumbled.

Of course she didn't believe it. Jenny didn't believe in luck, not to the extent many others did, anyway. People could be lucky, but not things. A dress could not be unlucky any more than a rabbit's foot could be lucky. "What's the saying?" she murmured aloud, eyeing her reflection in the mirror. "The rabbit's foot wasn't too lucky for the rabbit?"

Jenny set to work twisting and contorting her body, and eventually she managed all but two of the buttons. Grimacing, she gave the taffeta a jerk and felt the dress fall free even as she heard the buttons plunk against the floor.

While she gave little credit to luck, she did believe rather strongly in fate. As she stepped out of the wedding gown and donned her own dress, she considered the role fate had played in leading her to this moment. It was fate that she'd chosen to make Fort Worth her home. Fate that the Baileys had chosen her to make the dress. Fate that the brides had suffered accidents.

The shop's bell sounded. "*Now* someone comes," she whispered grumpily. "Not while I'm stuck in a five-hundred-dollar dress and needing assistance." She stooped to pick the buttons up off the floor and immediately felt contrite. She'd best be grateful for any customer, and besides, she welcomed the distraction from her troublesome thoughts.

Pasting a smile on her face, Jenny exited the dressing room and spied Mr. Trace McBride entering her shop.

He was dressed in work clothes—black frock jacket and black trousers, white shirt beneath a gold satin vest. He carried a black felt hat casually in his hand and raked a hand nervously through thick, dark hair.

Immediately, she ducked back behind the curtain.

Oh, my. Her heart began to pound. Why would the one man in Fort Worth, Texas, who stirred her imagination walk into her world at this particular moment?

She swallowed hard as she thought of her mother's advice. It was a crazy thought. Ridiculous.

But maybe, considering the stakes, it wouldn't hurt to explore the idea. Jenny had the sudden image of herself clothed in the Bad Luck Wedding Dress, standing beside Trace McBride, his three darling daughters looking on as she repeated vows to a preacher.

Her mouth went dry. Hadn't she sworn to fight for Fortune's Design? Wasn't she willing to do whatever it took to save her shop? If that meant marriage, well . . .

Wasn't it better to give up the dream of true love than the security of her independence?

Jenny stared at her reflection in the mirror. What would it hurt to explore her mother's idea? She wouldn't be committing to anything.

Jenny recalled the lessons she'd learned at Monique's knees. Flirtation. Seduction. That's how it was done. She took a deep breath. Was she sure about this? Could she go through with it? She *was* Monique Day's daughter. Surely that should count for something. She could do this.

Maybe.

Trace McBride. What did she really know about him? He was a businessman, saloon keeper, landlord, father. His smile made her warm inside and the musky, masculine scent of him haunted her mind. Once when he'd taken her arm in escort, she couldn't help but notice the steel of his muscles beneath the cover of his coat. His fingers would be rough against the softness of her skin. His kiss would be—

Jenny startled. Oh, bother. Had she lost her sense entirely?

Perhaps she had. She was seriously considering her mother's idea.

What was she thinking? He'd never noticed her before; what made her think he'd notice her now? What made her think he'd even consider such a fate as marriage?

Fate. There was that word again.

Was Trace McBride her fate? Could he save her from the rumor of the Bad Luck Wedding Dress? Could he help her save Fortune's Design?

She wouldn't know unless she did a little exploring. Was she brave enough, woman enough, to try?

She was Jenny Fortune. What more was there to say?

Taking a deep breath, Jenny pinched her cheeks, fluffed her honey-colored hair, and walked out into the shop.

Official Rules — No Purchase Necessary

To enter the sweepstakes outlined below, you must respond by the date specified and follow all entry instructions published elsewhere in this offer.

Dream Come True Sweepstakes

Sweepstakes begins 9/1/94, ends 1/15/96. To qualify for the Early Bird Prize, entry must be received by the date specified elsewhere in this offer. Winners will be selected in random drawings on 2/29/96 by an independent judging organization whose decisions are final. Early Bird winner will be selected in a separate drawing from among all qualifying entries.

Odds of winning determined by total number of entries received. Distribution not to exceed 300 million.

Estimated maximum retail value of prizes: Grand (1) $25,000 (cash alternative $20,000); First (1) $2,000; Second (1) $750; Third (50) $75; Fourth (1,000) $50; Early Bird (1) $5,000. Total prize value: $86,500.

Automobile and travel trailer must be picked up at a local dealer; all other merchandise prizes will be shipped to winners. Awarding of any prize to a minor will require written permission of parent/guardian. If a trip prize is won by a minor, s/he must be accompanied by parent/legal guardian. Trip prizes subject to availability and must be completed within 12 months of date awarded. Blackout dates may apply. Early Bird trip is on a space available basis and does not include port charges, gratuities, optional shore excursions and onboard personal purchases. Prizes are not transferable or redeemable for cash except as specified. No substitution for prizes except as necessary due to unavailability. Travel trailer and/or automobile license and registration fees are winners' responsibility as are any other incidental expenses not specified herein.

Early Bird Prize may not be offered in some presentations of this sweepstakes. Grand through third prize winners will have the option of selecting any prize offered at level won. All prizes will be awarded. Drawing will be held at 204 Center Square Road, Bridgeport, NJ 08014. Winners need not be present. For winners list (available in June, 1996), send a self-addressed, stamped envelope by 1/15/96 to: Dream Come True Winners, P.O. Box 572, Gibbstown, NJ 08027.

The Following Applies to the Sweepstakes Above:

No purchase necessary. No photocopied or mechanically reproduced entries will be accepted. Not responsible for lost, late, misdirected, damaged, incomplete, illegible, or postage-die mail. Entries become the property of sponsors and will not be returned.

Winner(s) will be notified by mail. Winner(s) may be required to sign and return an affidavit of eligibility/release within 14 days of date on notification or an alternate may be selected. Except where prohibited by law, entry constitutes permission to use of winners' names, hometowns, and likenesses for publicity without additional compensation. Void where prohibited or restricted. All federal, state, provincial, and local laws and regulations apply.

All prize values are in U.S. currency. Presentation of prizes may vary; values at a given prize level will be approximately the same. All taxes are winners' responsibility.

Canadian residents, in order to win, must first correctly answer a time-limited skill testing question administered by mail. Any litigation regarding the conduct and awarding of a prize in this publicity contest by a resident of the province of Quebec may be submitted to the Regie des loteries et courses du Quebec.

Sweepstakes is open to legal residents of the U.S., Canada, and Europe (in those areas where made available) who have received this offer.

Sweepstakes in sponsored by Ventura Associates, 1211 Avenue of the Americas, New York, NY 10036 and presented by independent businesses. Employees of these, their advertising agencies and promotional companies involved in this promotion, and their immediate families, agents, successors, and assignees shall be ineligible to participate in the promotion and shall not be eligible for any prizes covered herein. SWP 3/95